THE LIONHEADS

★ ★

THE LIONHEADS

a novel

Josiah Bunting

GEORGE BRAZILLER•NEW YORK

For Diana

Foreword

THIS BOOK IS a novel, not a history. It is about some soldiers serving in Vietnam in 1968.

What I observed during my own tour of duty there provides some of the background for the story: the geography, the organization of military units, the "hardware," some of the tactics. But the characters and the story are fictional. Any resemblance to men surviving or dead is coincidental.

The "Twelfth Infantry Division"—the "Lionheads" of the title—is also fictional. No Twelfth Division fought in Vietnam as part of the American Army. Similarly the directives, operations orders, the formal battle analyses, the combat "after-action" reports, the appendices, and map are fictional. On one occasion I quote from a report I wrote about the enemy's motives for his TET offensive. There is also an "Intelligence Bulletin" which describes the terrain and weather of one of the provinces of South Vietnam. The description is accurate, but the remainder of the Bulletin—describing a Viet Cong unit—is fictional.

Remember that the "events" described in the book take place in the Spring of 1968. The Army that fought then is not the same Army fighting now. There was no serious drug problem then, for example. We knew of no "massacre" in our part of Vietnam—in the Delta. It was the period of TET and just afterwards, and the American Army fought with distinction in executing its counteroffensive. So we believed then, and so I believe now, at least of the Division with which I served—the Ninth Infantry Division.

I have great affection and respect for the American G.I. who fought in Vietnam in those days. I remember being at a riverine fire base one day during TET, standing with my back to a late afternoon sun and observing part of an infantry company waiting to be picked up and "re-inserted" into the combat area. The troops I looked at had been fighting almost continuously for five days. Unconsciously they had arranged themselves into clusters of four or five —some standing, some kneeling with their weapons like ballplayers waiting to bat, others lying down, propped on their elbows, talking. In the bright sunlight they stood out against the river: relaxed, filthy, sunburned, at once bone-tired and alert, proud.

They were utterly American, as American as a tall man with a crew cut appears to a European: casual, loose-jointed, confident. They knew what was coming. Almost half their company had already been killed or wounded, and they were going back for more because they were ordered to.

The thing that got you was that last year they had been taking cars apart in Pittsfield or driving tractors outside Bismarck or sinking jump-shots in the gym in Cedar Rapids. Though the connotations of "Vietnam" had long since begun to widen, they had not thought too much about the war; and in any case the chances of their serving in Vietnam, as they gauged them at the time, were fairly remote.

But they didn't do well on their college boards, perhaps, or they said the hell with it, let's go in the service and then college afterwards, or a local judge posed a stern alternative to a stiff fine or thirty days on the county farm, or they were simply swept up in the draft. Then they went to Fort Riley or Fort Polk or Fort Dix, soldiered a bit in the States, read a skin-book going over on the plane, landed at Bien Hoa, and joined their units. Then they fought.

Most of them fought well, too. Most came home safely. Now they are in college or working or looking for a job. But when company comes they don't run upstairs to get their pictures or medals. They have put away their experience.

Many died. And of these, many died uncomprehending. They might have had a notion about stopping Communism (for example, the father of the private in this book tells his wife the Reds must not be allowed to get onto the Golden Gate Bridge) or of the necessity for killing off the vicious VC, but mainly they died because they felt obliged to be brave in the presence of their buddies, and, being brave, they were often exposed to enemy fire.

The officers who led them and those who presently officer the Army are generally worthy of such men as these. I have been privileged to know some of them well, and I would like to set down their names here in friendship and respect: James Morrison, Jim Barber, Ed Deagle, Pete Dawkins, Bill Stofft.

These men are worthy heirs to the tradition of Washington and Lee and Marshall, men who know their business, and who, because they hate war, have soldiered well.

J. B.

West Point
September 9, 1971

I saw the way things were going, a long time back. I said nothing. I'm one of the innocents who could have spoken up and out when no one would listen to the "guilty," but I did not speak and thus became guilty myself.

RAY BRADBURY
Fahrenheit 451

The abuse of greatness is when it disjoins Remorse from power.

Julius Caesar, II, 1

ONE

Division

General. Yes, I am a Major-General!
Samuel. For he is a Major-General!
All. He is! Hurrah for the Major-General!
General. And it is—it is a glorious thing
To be a Major-General!

W. S. GILBERT
The Pirates of Penzance

★1★

ENNOBLEMENT is earned by merit in the American Army. The depleted ranks of peers are annually replenished by fresh appointments from the ranks of its higher squirearchy, the appointments being made from a list annually prepared in the pentagonal Camelot. It is co-option with a courtly vengeance; and the new peers, the brigadiers and major generals, assume their mantles and styles with the guarded zest of the most sensitive parvenu. George, earl of Lemming, *Regis Gratia* Major General; *Honoris Causa,* long and distinguished service as measured by its acceptability to those who command the armed hosts of the Republic.

Among these senior warriors, a major general commanding a division in Vietnam is an earl, a Marcher Lord, and he maintains a briefing-court, a formal masculine assembly which meets regularly and according to a fixed protocol to enable him to take counsel

3

of his greater feudatories and his household knights. All here is order, degree, heraldry, pomp, deference.

The walls of the briefing-chamber: each panel of varnished plywood is emblazoned with the style of a brigade or battalion commanded by a viscount-colonel or a baron-lieutenant colonel of the Division. In the center of each panel is the head of a leopard or a coiled dragon snorting fire or castellated bricked towers or locked scimitars. And on these crests the banners, flared, warn and proclaim: *Primus Inter Pares; Essayons; Fear Naught; Semper Superba; Second to None!*

Presently it is whispered that General Lemming's progress has reached the foyer just without. A lieutenant gives voice to the intelligence: "Gentlemen, the Commanding General!" The fifty Lords-attendant rise as one, and slowly, deliberately, George Simpson Lemming and his suite enter the briefing-room. The Lords-attendant, ranged front to back according to their degrees and qualities, become the objects of his composed and benignant attention as he makes his way, deliberately, to his seat. Before turning to sit, he vouchsafes his rare and canny smile, looks on either side of him to ascertain that his immediate party are also prepared to sit, and then, without further ceremony, he sprawls into his 1953 brown barcalounger.

He does sprawl, too. His feet are lifted to the edge of the dais directly before his chair, and both his hands come up, their fingers extended to accommodate his cheekbones. All but the indirect stage lights are dimmed, and there is a scraping of chairs behind him as the fifty resume their seats. Now he turns his head

4

slowly—as someone once said of Churchill—like the gun-turret of a tank, toward the great podium on the right side of the stage, and his eyes travel up from the Lionhead and the NEMO ME IMPUNE LACESSIT inscribed on the front of the podium, and over it to the anxious face behind. He nods to the briefing officer, and the business begins.

"Good morning, Sir," the staff briefer says. "Enemy activity since 1800 hours yesterday continued at a relatively low level. No major contact by GVN or American forces was reported in the Republic of South Vietnam. In the Division AO, at 2115 last night at *this* location (the PFC assisting with the briefing indicates the location on the map with his pointer), 1st Battalion, 73rd Infantry, received eight rounds of 82mm mortar fire at Base Camp TARKENTON. One individual was slightly wounded and returned to duty immediately. At 2230, at *this* location (the PFC slides his pointer to the spot), Company B, 2nd Battalion, 73rd Infantry, received an unknown number of sniper rounds from a treeline approximately 500 meters east of its night position. There were no casualties. First Battalion, 21st Artillery, fired into the suspected enemy location in support, and the sniper fire ceased immediately. At 0145 hours, the Division Base received thirty-eight rounds of mixed 120mm and 82mm mortar fire from a location believed to be 2800 meters south. No damage to buildings or equipment was reported; one officer was slightly wounded . . ."

Here Lemming's officers permit themselves to laugh unguardedly, and they can see from the movement

5

of the backs of his ears that he too finds the incident not undeserving of mirth. For the Deputy G-1, a superannuated major, has received (in the mortar attack), a small piece of shrapnel in his buttocks while running through the doorway of a bunker. He is to leave on R & R—to meet his wife in Honolulu—this afternoon.

"How's Paulsen going to sit all the way to Hawaii?" the General asks.

"How's he going to function once he gets there?" the G-3 wonders aloud, greatly daring. A fresh wave of laughter, somewhat more than the incident warrants, rocks the officers near enough to share in the exchange.

High seriousness returns immediately and the briefing continues.

PFC Compella notes that the officers take no notice of him, but follow only the movements of the tip of his pointer as it plots the new locations on the briefing-map. It is a good opportunity for the freeborn yeoman to study the great nobleman among his own people. Indeed Compella's temporary assignment to the Division Headquarters Company—a rare stroke of good fortune, if only for a few days—gives him a chance offered few young soldiers new to Vietnam. The regular G-3 gopher, who had also distinguished himself as briefing-pointer, was home on emergency leave, and a call had gone out to the Division's Young Lion Academy (in which all new enlisted men and junior officers received ten days of combat orientation before being sent down to battalions) for a temporary replacement. A "real sharp individual" was specified, and Compella, who still had scalp showing above the ears from his

6

last haircut at home in Torrington, and a well-fitting set of new jungle fatigues into the bargain, was tapped.

"When I read out the location on the map," the Major had said at their rehearsal for the briefing at 0530 that morning, "you hit that acetate like a nurse puts a scalpel in the hands of a surgeon."

"At 310 hours, at *this* location, 1st Battalion, 73rd Infantry, received ten more rounds of 82mm mortar fire from a location immediately pinpointed by counter-mortar radar. First Battalion, 21st Artillery, took the targeted site under fire and no more rounds were received . . ."

So it continues for several more minutes, the Major crisply reciting his facts, Compella plopping his extended telescope pointer onto the designated locations (like a nurse puts a scalpel in the hands of a surgeon), the feudatories and household retainers either absorbed in what is said or affecting rapt attention, General Lemming staring at the map, and his immediate suite surreptitiously looking over at him to observe his reactions. But he does not often visibly react.

A pattern emerges from what is briefed, a pattern subtly different from what a competent tactician can infer from last night's up-date briefing, just as that was subtly different from what was briefed twelve hours before. With the exception of Lemming and two or three others, however, most of the officers of the Lionhead Division staff only vaguely understand what is meant, what is implied by the shifting enemy dispositions, the new sightings of hostile activity, the apparently random mortar barrages—only vaguely understand, or are no longer listening, or privately force themselves into some easy resolution, some glibly self-satisfying reduction to order of the various bits of information the Major and his successors at the podium broadcast to them.

But there is a talent, a mentality found in very few officers, which in the Clausewitzian idiom "powerfully apprehends," easily and quickly, the nature of the enemy's freshly modified dispositions and his changing order of battle. George Lemming has it unquestionably.

He still sprawls in the huge chair, in appearance amused, disdainful, calm. He interrupts only rarely. But his perceptions—when he gives voice to them—are so incisive that they immediately light up the huge mapped landscape for the rest. He asks the briefers questions that elicit useful answers. He is a skilled examiner but his assumptions and methods are not Socratic. He is at times remorselessly blunt, grunting splenetically at questions misunderstood or answers unsatisfactory. He remembers a professor at the War College telling him in jest that an examiner of students should work like a fine dentist: locating the cavities and decay without giving pain. But that is not quite his way either. Through long usage he has come to learn that the confident young men who recite the daily litany of military information have little idea of the import of their statements. They feed him information: *he* must evoke the necessary conclusions from his own intellectual resources. *He* must supply the answers, shredding the egos of his senior staff when their dribbling nervous suggestions are made, causing them to extenuate their stupidity afterwards by admiring comments about the quality of his tactical gifts.

The staff colleges, the advanced courses, the specialty schools, even the curriculum at West Point have all trained their students to answer quickly: any solution is better than no solution. One must learn to think, to "function" under great pressure, to preserve an inner core of tranquillity, to factor out the superficial and grasp the essence of the question posed and "generate" an answer to it. Any answer is better than no answer. But the General, reflecting on these matters, thinks only: "That's bullshit." Not bullshit for Andy Goodpaster or Tick Bonesteel or George Marshall, but for the officers he has working for him at Division, yes, it is absurd. A mule, Frederick the Great wrote, can accompany his master on many campaigns: but he is still a mule at the end of the war.

Suddenly he breaks in: "Where's the 317th MF Battalion, Major?"

"Well, G-2 has sightings at *this* location," the officer answers, PFC Compella tapping the acetate, "and down here, and here, and here. The sightings seem to come farther south day by day. But I couldn't say for sure where they are now . . ."

"Guess."

The Major clears his throat, playing for time. He guesses.

Lemming's jaws clench. He purses his lips. He is not pleased. The General wants informed conjecture, imaginative solutions. He looks over at the Major's superior —the G-3 sitting two seats to his left. He tells him

9

quietly to "do something about the fucking major."

More officer-briefers follow, Compella moving to the side of the platform away from the podium as new chart-bearers and pointers take his place. On come the briefers, captains and lieutenants and majors, the G-4, the G-5, the surgeon, the chaplain, and finally a gross porcine functionary called the Red Cross Man. Between him and Lemming there is as much *simpatico* as between the captain of wrestling and the class poet.

"Last week Red Cross teams assigned to the Division made thirty-seven visits to battalion and company base camps. They distributed 1232 ditty bags, 20,000 courtesy packets of Salem cigarettes contributed by Braniff International, and 4600 cups of Kool-Aid. The Division office processed 126 cablegrams to hometown Red Cross field representatives and helped arrange fifty-five emergency leaves. Work on the new E.M. center continues. We hope to open the facility within fifteen working days and it will be able to serve 350 troops at once."

"What'll you have in there?"

"Yes, Sir. Ten table-tennis courts. A library of 1500 paperbacks. Six pool tables. Four television sets. Fifteen portable writing cubicles. Five large coffee urns and popcorn machines. Two jukeboxes and a donut dispenser."

"Suffering Christ," Lemming thinks. He purses his lips and raises his eyebrows in a way he hopes will seem to register approval and discourage further communication. It does. There remains only one more briefer, a member of his personal staff who announces the forthcoming visit of two reporters on a fact-finding mission, noting that the reporters are from Oklahoma and that they will be wanting to meet soldiers from that state. Now he nods down at the General and he and PFC Compella come to attention on the stage. The General disengages himself from the barcalounger and the metal chairs again grate as his retainers rise to acknowledge his intention to leave the briefing-room.

On the way out he tells the Assistant Chief of Staff to have the 1st Brigade commander, the G-2, and the G-3 come in to see him after lunch, and he congratulates the G-3 and the Chief of Staff on the general excellence of the briefings, except for—he nods conspiratorially— the defective hypothesizing of the one Major. Going into the foyer he stops, turns around, and looks back at the stage.

"Who's that new kid with the pointer?"

"PFC Compella, Sir." (Can't you read his nametape, my Lord?)

"Just report in?"

"Yes, Sir," the G-3 answers.

"Nice-looking boy."

"Yes, sir. Good-morning, Sir."

AFTER the morning briefings General Lemming feeds well and carefully in the Senior Officers' Mess: grapefruit, black coffee, two pieces of toast evenly spread with Cross and Blackwell marmalade, one fried egg, and a 500mg ascorbic acid pill. The cooks and steward expect him at 0815, and unless the briefing has been unexpectedly long he is unvaryingly on time to the minute. He sits alone at the far end of the mess, under a large Remington picture showing a cavalryman using his dead mount as a prop for his rifle. The aide and the Chief of Staff break his solitude only on matters of great urgency.

General Lemming likes to ease into the day and keep to a regular pattern of activity.

Kowalski wakes him each morning in the comfortable air-conditioned trailer he occupies near the headquarters building: "General, General . . . 0630, Sir," he says, noting the number of Lark cigarette butts in the ashtray by the bed, and where in the volume of military history the place-mark has been stuck. While

Lemming takes his shower Kowalski checks to see how many pages the General has read the night before and guesses at his forthcoming testiness or civility from this. If there has been a mortar attack on the Division Base the night before, the General will be in a filthy mood; he has never been a sound sleeper, and ten or fifteen rounds of 82mm on the base at 3 A.M. will keep him up reading until 4:30.

By 7 A.M. he has shaved and dressed himself in the starched, beautifully faded jungle fatigues and spit-shined boots Kowalski has laid out on the bed. The sleeves of the fatigue jacket are always rolled over exactly five times, each roll 2½ inches wide, so that the sleeves fall perfectly above the break of his elbows.

For twenty minutes Lemming works at the desk in his sitting-room in the trailer, keeping his personal affairs tidy, writing curt notes to his broker at Kidder, Peabody, or letters of reassurance to his wife Katherine and his sons. At 0720 there is a knock, the door opens, and the Aide-de-Camp, Captain Terwilliger, announces the time. If it has been a good night, Lemming asks him to wait for him inside; if not, "I'll be out in a minute, Terwilliger." And soon he rises from his desk, fits the green baseball cap onto his head—noting the symmetry of the fit in the mirror—and joins the aide for the short walk to the briefing-room.

He walks like a middle-aged actor trying to walk like an old Indian chief: deliberately, slowly, head thrown back, hands clasped over his spine. Again, if he is in a civil mood, he will make small talk with the aide: "Sleep well, Paul?" "Yes, Sir." "Red Cross girls last night?" (sidelong glance, activity at the corners of the mouth). "Not *last* night, General."

He then attends the morning briefing, has breakfast, and works in his office for two hours, granting interviews, planning the day's activities with his personal staff, working over his own 1:100,000 map, making calls to Field Force, giving orders, handing out awards to departing officers and NCO's of the Division Headquarters. The awards he contemptuously calls "goodies," feeling that awards for service should not be given men who have excelled in their staff or command positions: "The only perquisite of an officer's assignment is a clean efficiency report." But he usually endorses the awards recommendations anyway; the officers who work for him should not be penalized because the other divisions are so liberal in handing out decorations.

Lemming's desk is covered with the carefully arranged souvenirs of a career officer of some wit, the materials diagrammed by Sergeant Kowalski so that they can be put back properly each evening after the desk has been dusted and polished. These include: a pencil receptacle covered with a cracked tiny reproduction of Gainsborough's *Blue Boy* (Fortnum and Mason, London, a gift from a former Sandhurst faculty member with whom he once served on a Joint Staff); several carved ivory elephants (the Wake PX, between flights); a small bronze Balinese dancer (Bangkok, 1963, on leave); two porcelain elephants; a leaden fist with its third finger sticking up, placed to discomfit whoever is standing at attention before the desk, and bearing the inscription: "Your dime, start talking"; two swagger sticks given him by Vietnamese generals he despises; a cigarette box with a handsome crest (2nd Battalion, 54th Infantry, 1942); half a—can it be?—human skull—no, no, only an old coconut shell; an ashtray wrought from the casing of a 105mm artillery round, dazzlingly polished and suitably inscribed as the "10,000th round fired by the 1st Battalion, 19th Artillery"; and a Brooks Brothers executive calendar bound in fine Morocco.

Each of these trinkets—and he has hundreds more at home in Sequenoy—reminds him of some aspect, some assignment in the career which he now regards as beginning to fulfill its promise.* He well knows that commanding a Division in the combat theater can be the capstone of an excellent career of service, leading to one further assignment—probably to a continental Army command as Deputy Commanding General, without promotion; or, if he truly distinguishes himself as Division Commander, the assignment will lead to another promotion—the big step to three stars (only 15 percent of two-star generals are promoted to three-star rank) and perhaps assignment to command a Corps or be a Deputy Chief of Staff on the Army Staff in Washington. Lemming loves his farmhouse in Sequenoy, but he has no intention of retiring into the Shenandoah in the next few years. He wants to be Chief of Staff—of the Army.

He lacks command presence despite his formidable, badly distributed size (6′ 2½″, 210 pounds). He knows this, and recognizes that he has achieved his current

* For the entry on General Lemming in Flett's *Register of Professional Soldiers of NATO Signatories* for January 1968 see Appendix I, p. 211.

coveted appointment by a reputation for raw physical courage and a mind that cuts to the core of tactical and logistical problems and can rapidly develop workable solutions to them. He is utterly without remorse or sentimentality and has little time for soldiers who betray their emotions. His character is cold, his insights keen, his mind relentlessly logical.

As to hobbies, he has few. He favors military fiction and military history for reading: the novels of Captain Marryat; the works of C. S. Forester (not including *The General,* which he regards as a spiteful book); Fortescue's *History of the British Army* (all thirteen volumes crated and shipped with him to the Twelfth Division); Colonel John Thomason's reminiscences about the Marine Corps in the old days; Holland Rose's *Napoleon;* Freeman's *Lee's Lieutenants;* Henderson's *Stonewall Jackson* (his favorite book); Churchill's *History of the English-Speaking Peoples.*

He keeps a small record collection in his trailer, indulging himself nightly in the composers he calls "the controlled romantics": Mendelssohn, some Schumann, Schubert. He will have no truck with Tschaikovsky or Borodin or Rachmaninoff.

Lemming is a crony. The men he knew at Benning in the mid-thirties are now retired to Warrenton or La Jolla or have become general officers. He keeps up with the latter: in letters, at reunions, in the Army-Navy Journal. Some of these are already lieutenant generals, one even a four-star general, all of them placed where they can do him good or harm. Phil Regan, another Virginian, commands CDC and is a great gadgeteer. He sends new weapons and vehicles to the 12th Division for field-combat trials, and Lemming sees that they get a fair tryout, whatever his reservations about their prospective utility in the combat zone. Zorin Rockacre, whose father Lemming was once an aide for, commands II Field Force—the Army Corps to which the Twelfth Division is assigned. He too is a crony with whom Lemming is completely at ease, to whom he can confide his reservations or endorsements of projected plans. But only up to a point. There comes a time, late in the evenings in the air-conditioned trailers filled with cigar smoke, when Lemming eventually accedes to Rockacre's wishes: "George, we've been friends a long time. You know when I'm serious about something. You've got to get your Third Brigade into Go Cong Province and clean up War Zone K. I know what your reservations are about it. But I've got to insist here . . ."

And "Right, Z, I'll do it."

He knows the superintendent of West Point and the Governor of Virginia; the Vice-Chief of Staff of the Army; COMUSARPAC; the Marine I Corps commander. It is his sensing of his standing in the eyes of men like these that ultimately dictates his selection of options.

He is a superb Division commander—for the infantry or armored infantry war in Europe in the 1940's. He fights in Vietnam using the methods that would have made him a successful and popular commander with his superiors and with the public in World War II. All of his instincts are to engage his enemy and destroy

17

him. No one does it better in Vietnam. His aides and principal staff marvel at his ability to infer from a developing enemy situation the certain whereabouts of enemy battalions two days ahead, and how rapidly he can figure counters to the enemy's moves.

On most days, for example, his chopper sets him down in front of Division at 1600 or 1700. He has been visiting his battalion and brigade base camps, overflying battles in progress, talking to officers of the Riverine Brigade at fire support bases. Totally at ease and alert, he walks slowly into his office, lays his holster on the sofa, turns around to be briefed by the Chief of Staff or his assistant. He wants to know what has happened in places he hasn't visited. He is told. He stares at his detailed wall map and says nothing for perhaps thirty seconds. Then, "OK. Tell Manley I want the 2nd of the 73rd unassed out of CONDOR (the name of a fire base that battalion is presently occupying) by 1830. I'll get Rockacre to spring loose an AHC to move them here. He fingers the map, shaking his wrist. That's where they (the VC) are. The 1st of the 21st can support them from Mo Dinh. Have Manley put the 1st of the 73rd on standby. Where's Robertson's 1st Battalion? Good. Put them on standby . . ." etc.

For the staff it is a revelation. They are schoolboys again. "See, *ae* makes it the genitive case. *Da lucernam puellae mihi.* The lamp *of* the girl. See what I mean?" "Oh, yeah, now I understand: the *genitive* case." Like schoolboys the staff half wonders at, half hates the abilities of the teacher. How could he know so much, sort out the issues so fast? Experience? Brains? Instinct? Or is he just well organized?

It is all of these, and more. It is said that great leaders must be judged in part on their appointments to positions of trust and authority under them. The important generals of the modern West have almost always had efficient and responsive staffs. Lemming's is no exception. There is much sycophantism, of course. Those who are sycophants fancy they are not. They will innovate within the "parameters" which their experience with Lemming tells them are the final limits of accepted innovation. The General gives "mission-type" orders, allowing his staff to take what steps are necessary to fulfill their missions.

These steps, however, are always informed by a sense of what will please the General. "How would Lemming like me to do it? What will please him?" Those who gauge shrewdly what it is that will satisfy him are assured of his support and, more important to them, of good efficiency reports.

Lemming has a proper conceit of his abilities; he does not take to criticism. In assembling his principal staff he has selected those whose behavior will most purely reflect his will. Those who give him a bad time are dispatched to other, less prestigious commands.

Civilian observers are apt to be revolted when they see how the division bureaucracy operates. They notice that when the Assistant Division Commanders and the Chief of Staff talk with him, they search his face carefully, watching his eyes and lips; they listen raptly, catching the inflections of his voice. When they sense that his statements are building to a culmination, they begin nodding at him even before the last words are out of his mouth, showing their eagerness to please, to be thought to be in agreement. When he makes one of his rare jokes they begin to chuckle before the punch-line. "I think the little bastards have gone in here," he says, pointing to a green place on a map. He turns to Colonel Murphy, or whoever is with him, and by the time his eyes have lighted on the listener's face he can expect the listener will be nodding in agreement, quietly assenting. "Yes, Sir, that's a good point. Right. I see it now."

And yet the General dislikes obvious obsequiousness, so they have to be careful with him—not too eager, not too malleable, just enough. Rank and military usage are, of course, entirely on his side. The principal staff officers, not counting Colonel Murphy, a "full bull," are all lieutenant colonels on the make, most of them promoted early and eighteen or twenty years younger than Lemming. They dare not tell him to his face that they disagree with him. They can tell when he is speaking *ex cathedra,* and at such times they would no more contradict him than throw a grenade into his office. Those that have tried it soon leave the Lionhead Division. Lemming will call in Murphy and say, "Oh, Chuck, get that Colonel what's-his-name [he affects a certain vagueness as to the names of lesser mortals], ah, Colonel Kepler, and send the son-of-a-bitch down to IV Corps or up to MACV staff. I don't care which. Have Mason write him up for a bronze star for achievement, you know, let him down fairly light, but get him out of here." And then, two or three days later, he will scribble a few lines on the heretic's efficiency report which will assure he will never be promoted higher. Clever lines, too, pretending the most perfect disinterest.

For example:

> Kepler was a competent and brave battalion commander but he frankly lacks the qualities prerequisite to useful service on the general staff.

Or

> Lt-Colonel Newton, though he has made important contributions to the achievement of our counterinsurgency mission, lacked the vision to promote truly useful innovations in the G-5 area.

Not only are his staff afraid of him and anxious to advance their own careers; they are also tired. Some of them have worked for Lemming at Division for seven or eight months. There are no days off. They work from 0630 to 2200. On every third or fourth night the base camp is mortared, which means they average perhaps five hours sleep each night. Some of this time they squander drinking beer or writing letters or reading paperbacks. And all the time it is fiercely hot. What this comes down to is that his staff have become efficient and even capable projections of the will of Lemming. But, as in the case of Newton, they "lack the vision," or the freshness of understanding to perceive what has gone wrong, or the courage to point out what has gone wrong. They dream of a Legion of Merit and their wives in their arms at San Francisco in only two or three months. Why risk their careers and these glorious rewards for the sake of shooting off their mouths?

So: Lemming is a superb tactician and a leader who can expect that what he says will invariably be trans-

lated into policy. As for the hearts and minds of the
Vietnamese he flies over daily, he could not in truth care
less. He gives extraordinarily professional dinners and
cocktail parties for the Vietnamese generals and politi-
cians: flowers beautifully arranged, Cutty Sark, expen-
sive gifts (his tastes run to Japanese binoculars), Mekong
River shrimp as wide as flashlight batteries and
arranged in the shape of a Lionhead, four wine courses.
He visits Province and District chiefs and inquires about
their problems. Can he help? Has so-and-so's battalion
run a MED-CAP for you in the last month? How's your
little girl, Tranh, the one with malaria? Better? Wonderful. Give her my warm regards. Congratulations on
your Cross of Gallantry, Dinh. It is a high honor. Yes,
we can get our Rome plows to clear the jungle alongside the Cho Gao. I'll attend to it this afternoon.

But his heart is in none of this and he is unconvincing.

"OK, Terwillinger, let's get back to Division and
back to work. Good-bye, Dinh, and stay in touch. Let
us know what you need." All the while knowing that
in two or three days one of the hamlets Dinh "controls"
may have to be leveled because the VC are really
running it.

Perhaps Lemming's attitude toward his profession
and toward those who serve in his Division is best
expressed by the letter he has had laminated, framed,
and hung on the wall behind his desk. It is a letter sent
him by the parents of a young man, a private, recently
killed at TET. The parents wanted to share it with the
General. It had been written by their son's platoon
leader, a lieutenant himself later killed:

Please be assured Richard died like a man. He may not have believed in this war but I know for a fact he believed in being a man.

And so: up at 0630, personal affairs, formal briefings, breakfast, office work, flights over the battles and visits to base camps, luncheons with the Vietnamese and conversations with Province chiefs, back to Division for up-date briefings, to the Mess for two gin-and-tonics and dinner, the first ten minutes of the staff's nightly movie, twenty pages of *Lee's Lieutenants*, and then, if it has been a good day, to sleep.

Office of the Commanding General
Headquarters, Twelfth Infantry Division in Vietnam
0900 Hours, 12 March 1968

"MASON, have Sergeant Kowalski get some coffee, you know, and some of those cakes from the General's Mess; have him bring in a real nice spread."

The beneficiaries of the combat-zone *hors d'oeuvres* are already seated at the General's work-table at the far end of his office, in pleasant conversation with Lemming. The Chief of Staff returns to them, smiling. "Kowalski'll be right in, Sir."

"Thank you, Chuck," says the General. He nods somewhat curtly at the guests, indicating he wants them to get down to brass tacks. The man, tall and sandy-haired, begins:

"See, I'm not Robert Shaplen, and the constituency I write for is not Montgomery County or Grosse Pointe. I don't go in for that slick kind of reportage and my people wouldn't be sucked in by it. I know what you're doing here, General, and I can tell you that being here in a general's office is a privilege for me—and certainly for Betty. I know that TET business in the papers at home, most of the papers, was a bill of goods. What TET was like was the Battle of the Bulge. Like that. The VC made a big splash, like . . . they got in the Embassy garden in Saigon, just like the Germans accomplished tactical surprise at first—you know, they had on our uniforms and all. They mortared a few cities in the Delta and they killed a lot of ARVN. And of course up in Hué they massacred thousands of civilians. But the steam went out of it in a hurry, just like the steam went out of the German attack in 1944, whenever it was.

"The press at home made out like it was a VC victory. You know Art Buchwald? He compared General Westmoreland to General Custer. People get sucked in by that. Some of them even think it's funny. Well, Betty and I don't think it's funny. So what I want is your assessment of what the 12th Division did during that time. How long it took you to get your AO under control, and all—hell, you probably never *lost* control— and how the stories about the cities being blown up by us are inflated. That sort of thing."

He is from Tulsa, and his wife, who writes for the same paper, has come out with him on the pretext of wanting to gather information about the troops. As she says, "There's a lot of wives and mothers waiting for these kids." Neither of them has ever been outside the United States. To General Lemming and Colonel Murphy the intensity of their interest and enthusiasm seems both comical and admirable. They are obviously good grist.

MACV protocol has wasted no time getting them fitted out with new jungle fatigues—nametapes, patches and all, so that in appearance they might almost be taken for new recruits, but for the attractive "back porch" of Mrs. Maye, which even the baggy fatigue pants can't disguise, and the fact that Victor Maye is forty-six years old and writes a syndicated column run in eighty Midwest newspapers. Enthusiastic novices or not, they are to be taken with high seriousness.

The General clears his throat, looking pleasantly at his Chief of Staff: "Chuck, why don't you give them some statistics for a start and I can wrap up with an overview, kind of a broad-brush, later."

"Certainly, Sir."

The Chief strides to a wall map and begins pointing out cities and rivers in the Delta, reading the guests into the geography of Vietnam south of Saigon. The Mayes are raptly attentive. Lemming leans back in his chair, folds his hands across his stomach, and listens approvingly. What you needed, he reflects, was a Chief of Staff like Murphy, a regular man for all seasons, a man who can switch frequencies to accommodate any receiver: Joe Alsop, Dean Brelis, Scotty Reston, even rubes from Oklahoma.

"You see," the Chief begins, "what they did was to use a month, maybe, to infiltrate these cities in small groups. Most of them were indigenous VC; they had relatives in the cities who couldn't very well throw them out of their own houses. A lot of them grew up there. You know, imagine a carload of kids coming home to Tulsa from college. The VC are smart and patient. What they would do was to go out and link up with VC companies (the pointer flicks officiously all over the map) and get mortar rounds—maybe only one at a time—bandoliers, parts of rifles even, and infiltrate them in. Keep that up for a month, say 10,000 local VC doing that, and pretty soon they've got ten or fifteen cities ready to blow when they want. They don't have any artillery down here, nothing big; but they have B-40's, like rocket launchers, Chicom carbines, AK-47's—that's a good weapon but it's more useful up in I Corps than down here. On the first night of TET, on prior arrangement and probably using radio too, they started shooting. For example, local ARVN headquarters and outposts. Then they would occupy hospitals and schools and other buildings and wait for us to come and dig them out."

Victor Maye vaguely apprehends that B-40's and AK-47's are weapons. His wife does not. "They would occupy hospitals!" she exclaims. "What would they do to the patients in there?"

"They're smart, and remember they probably *knew* half the patients."

"What were the patients in there for?"

"Oh, a lot of things. Malnutrition. They have a bad diet. A lot of foot diseases."

Lemming, who knows the hospitals are mainly full of civilian casualties of war, says nothing.

"What would they do then?"

"They didn't have to do anything. Just wait. They

27

knew we'd have to find out where they were and have to clean them out of the buildings. They're patient, like I said. You probably know the joke about General Giap—he's their Chief of Staff—the joke about him and the private. One day Giap gives ten privates each an 82mm mortar round and tells them to carry them to the Mekong Delta from Hanoi. It takes them five months to get down there—down here, that is. Two privates, however, are killed by airstrikes, two more by booby-traps, another by a snake, three drown in a river, one is shot. The last one gets to the Delta, gives his mortar round to a VC supply sergeant and walks back home. He gets to Hanoi a year later and goes up to Giap. He tells him he delivered his Mortar round. 'Very nice,' Giap says. 'Here's another one. Get going.'" Remembering his Jean de Larteguy the Chief adds, "They're like ants."

"What kind of snakes are there?" Mrs. Maye wants to know.

"Oh, the usual spectrum of Asian pit-vipers," Colonel Murphy says, Lemming admiring his resourcefulness. "Tonkinese puffed adders, cobras, kraits. They bite you, you start saying your prayers on the spot. Don't bother with serum. Nothing can save you."

Ignoring his wife, Victor Maye asks impatiently, "How many did we kill?"

"General, correct me if I'm wrong, I haven't got the charts handy, but I think the division body-count during the week of TET was 3,200."

"All of those were certified VC—is that right, General Lemming?" Maye's pencil is poised over the steno pad in his lap.

28

"Most of them. Either VC or VC sympathizers."

"How many did the Division lose?"

"Well, counting an ARVN battalion we had attached to us at the time, 78 dead and 340 wounded."

Maye looks at his wife. He shakes his head slowly from side to side, like a child admiring a new Schwinn. "That's some casualty ratio," he says. "What did we get them with?"

The Chief of Staff goes back to the map. His pointer crackles the acetate and glides swiftly along the rivers and treelines. "This is where most of them went after they mortared the cities. We went in there with air-mobile and riverine and sealed them off. We got a lot of them this way. See, what we try to do is pinpoint their locations and seal them into the woodlines or anywhere they can't get out of. We have all these places under our artillery fans. Our infantry rarely moves out from under these fans."

He takes a piece of string off the shelf, loops one end around a red grease pencil, scales off the string to the range of a 105 battery, presses the other end of the string to the locations of the artillery batteries, and swings the grease pencil around his thumb in circles with a scaled radius of 9000 meters. Dates have already been placed on the map over points where "significant contacts" had been achieved.

"See, you get a fix on where they've gone—from local friendlies or from Airborne personnel detectors or visual contact. Then you seal them in there with infantry and then you call in 105's and air. After a few hours the companies make a sweep through the area."

Mrs. Maye is thinking now about the VC private with

the mortar round, the one sent down from Hanoi. "They don't care much about life, they're like the Chinese, isn't that right?"

"Well, sometimes it looks like that, doesn't it, Sir?" Colonel Murphy might be a Big Ten football coach whose team has just beaten Swarthmore in an exhibition game: We just do our job, Ma'am.

Lemming says nothing, but nods sagely. He never trusts reporters fully.

"What would happen when they did that in the cities?" asks Mrs. Maye.

"Did what?"

"Went in there or got chased in there, like they were chased into the woodlines?" From where she is sitting she can just make out the woodlines the Chief's pointer has traced, breaking the monotony of white on the map like strokes of pale-green watercolor. She has flown over the Upper Delta once, and because looking down out of the slick made her nauseous she had read a MACV fact sheet most of the way. She has an idea that "wood-line" denotes a neatly defined grove of pine or spruce, still dry at this time of year. Clearly the explosions of artillery and "air" must have turned them into raging furnaces. As for the cities, she wonders about the VC holing up in the hospitals, holding guns on the people with malnutrition, whether they were burned up, too. But they don't value life the way we do.

"Well, of course, that was the crunch. But you see that's how things get twisted up in the States. We had an Air Force major attached to a battalion, an air controller. He went into one of the cities with the battalion

30

that had to clear out the VC who were holed up in there, and he was the one who made the crack about having to destroy the city to save it. That's the kind of thing—*Time* gets it, or somebody, and they just print a bald story and never say anything about what could have happened if the VC had stayed in there, if we hadn't gotten them out."

Mrs. Maye has a vision of groups of Asiatics in black tunics, sitting in small orderly groups with their arms wrapped around their knees. They are being lectured to and converted to Communism by commissars in Astrakhans.

"So what *did* you do to get them out?" her husband breaks in.

"We went in with infantry and went through the city block by block, clearing buildings and houses. We used air only when we had to, when it was plain there was no other way to get them out without taking unacceptable friendly casualties."

"Was the city destroyed?" He looks at the General.

Lemming closes his eyes and nods, pretty bad.

"Are there any VC left in there now?"

"Not enough to matter."

"General, what is your overall assessment of the results of the TET offensive?"

"Well, they did achieve both tactical and strategic surprise. You know, it was a truce period, but that doesn't stop these people. We had an idea they might make a few moves, shoot up an outpost, perhaps, but nothing like what they did. We had a whole brigade deployed to the west, way up near the border, to interdict their resupply. But this is the kind of thing they're good at. They planned it so that when we came to get them out of the cities they could point to us and say to the people, see, that's what the Americans are doing to your cities and villages. These people are cagey, determined, and—like the Chief says—patient.

"The Asiatic mind discounts death," Maye says. "I mean they all go to Nirvana, they think. Isn't that right? They're prepared to take serious casualties, even disastrous ones by our standards?"

The General, who takes second place to no one in caginess, is starting to get unaccountable vibrations. He looks pointedly over his glasses at Colonel Murphy and back at Maye. "Well, let's say they will take heavy losses if they think they can make us look bad," he says. Until now he has been the soul of graciousness, granting a long interview to a couple of reporters from the sticks who would ordinarily have been foisted off on the Assistant Chief of Staff or the PIO. Suddenly he is impatient. He has less chemistry with Tulsa, it seems, than he has with the *Time*, Inc., people. He walks over to his desk, presses the intercom, and calls for his aide.

"Captain Terwilliger has something for you, a little memento of your visit with us."

The aide comes in, hands him two zippo-sized packages, which he gives to the reporters. "This is a little thing we had made up for us in Japan."

They open the boxes and fondle the lighters, each with the Lionhead crest and the motto NEMO ME IMPUNE LACESSIT.

"Goddamit, General, this is awfully kind of you," Maye says. On an impulse his wife reaches out and takes Lemming's right hand between both of hers. "God bless you," she says, and joins her husband and the aide to go on a tour of the Tactical Operations Center.

The Chief gets up to leave also. There are other visitors to get ready for. "No problem with the woman," he says to the General. "Probably he's alright too."

Lemming says nothing, smiles his inscrutable smile, and returns to his desk.

★4★

Office of the Commanding General
Headquarters, Twelfth Infantry Division in Vietnam
0930 Hours, 12 March 1968

"MASON, getchure ass in here!"

The Assistant Chief of Staff is reading *David Copper-field* at his desk in the outer office of Division Head-quarters. As bidden, he rises and goes into the Chief of Staff's office, immediately next to General Lemming's.

"Yes, Sir?"

"We got two people coming in here at ten, I think you know about it, for the General to give solatium payments to. Have Sergeant Kowalski get a couple of cartons of Salems, a tray of cookies, and some soft drinks, ah, coffee, and some Division yearbooks." He presses the tips of the fingers of his left hand with the index finger of his right as he enumerates the items. "Let's see, and take the goddamn artillery-shell ash-trays out, in case they come in here. And get rid of these pictures." (Colonel Murphy has been scrutinizing

34

photos of the damage wrought by a recent B-52 strike.)

"Nice snapshots, Sir. They made a desert and called it peace."

"Wha-at?"

"Tacitus."

"Goddamit, Mason, you still reading that shit on duty?"

"No, Sir."

The Major leaves Colonel Murphy and passes along his instructions to Kowalski and the enlisted men idling in the hallway.

"Has the G-1 brought the money over here?" Colonel Murphy shouts from his office.

"Yes, Sir," Mason calls back.

"How much?"

"7000 piastres, Sir. Sixty dollars U.S. equivalent."

"Good."

At 1400 a jeep pulls up in front of the Headquarters building and two Vietnamese get out. The husband is about forty-five, a tiny wizened man who looks around apprehensively before joining his wife and the captain escorting them as they walk under the Lionhead crest over the door. Hearing them in the hall, Mason alerts the Chief of Staff and the General, both of whom are therefore standing expectantly in the door of the General's office as the party turns in from the hall. Colonel Murphy walks up to the Vietnamese, bobbing his head up and down.

"Mr. and Mrs. Tranh, we are *so* pleased you've been able to get over here." He puts out his hand for the husband to shake and gestures with his left arm for

35

them to come ahead. Noting that the clerks have stopped typing and are staring at them he makes a rapid circular motion with his hand and shoots them a fierce glance. Get back to work, goddamit! The party goes into Lemming's office and are seated around his coffee table. The guests look at the General expectantly.

"Mr. Tranh, this is a great tragedy you've sustained, and we know what a blow it is for you. It's something we feel terrible about here. We want you to know that we have made arrangements with Captain Kramer to see that you get every assistance rebuilding your house. And it's terrible, a terrible shame about your son. I know how much you must have loved him. I have two sons of my own."

It is true. The General has two sons: one at Woodberry Forest, another at Carleton College. He has just given the latter a new Mustang.

"You have son too?"

"Yes, two fine boys. I'm very proud of them."

"How old they?"

"One is fourteen, one is nineteen."

"In Army?"

The General smiles thinly, solicitously. No, not now. Not yet.

"Long way!" Tranh smiles and gestures at the big globe next to the sofa.

"Yes." Lemming and the Chief of Staff agree on that.

"You see them soon?"

"Perhaps in a few months."

Sergeant Kowalski comes in with the tray and offers soft drinks to the guests. The Vietnamese accept them but put them down on the table. Kowalski takes the Salems and places them on the sofa next to Mrs. Tranh.

"The General feels terrible about this, every time it happens, and we try to make it up somehow although we know we can't." Colonel Murphy is in dead earnest. "But we have a very small token for you, Mr. Tranh. We know it's only a fraction of what could mean anything to you." Suddenly he remembers his Lincoln from the Academy: "Nothing could beguile you from a loss as overwhelming as this one is." Lemming reflects—without the expression on his face changing—that he has never heard such language out of Colonel Murphy before. Jesus!

The husband takes the envelope with the solatium payment inside. The Lionhead crest is embossed on the upper left corner, and typewritten in capital letters and carefully centered on the envelope is the epigraph: FROM THE MEN OF THE TWELFTH INFANTRY DIVISION IN DEEP CONDOLENCE. The mother weeps silently.

For once both Lemming and his Chief of Staff are at a loss. Tranh and his wife both move as if to get up.

"Would you like something to eat? To drink?"

"No," Tranh says. He is smiling at them.

They all walk slowly out of General Lemming's office, the clerk-typists not stopping this time, the General and the Chief both accompanying them all the way to the jeep. In their absence a trailer has been attached to it, filled with tools, burlap sacks of rice, and some cartons of C-rations. Colonel Murphy points brightly at the gifts and Tranh nods in recognition.

"Thank you, Sir," he says, and they get into the jeep for the ride back to the foundation of their former home and the grave nearby.

Colonel Murphy returns to his office and resumes business.

"How'd it go, Sir, OK?" Major Mason has brought in yet another armload of paperwork.

The Chief of Staff looks up at him, and because he feels good about what he has just done, he leans back in his office chair, puts his hands behind his head and says yes, it has all gone very well. "You know, Mason, these people have suffered terribly. And they're not on any pissy-ass one-year tour. They live through this war. They get wise to H and I fires but sometimes they get hurt. You gotny kids?"

"No, Sir."

"Well, losing a kid is the worst thing in your life. What can you say to people who have just had their son killed? I think it was their only son. Every time I see one of their kids wounded or even not wounded, just dirty and skinny—how they are, you know—I think of my kids in Chevy Chase and what *they* have to grow up with: good food, schools, sports, their own rooms. Parents who love them."

Mason stares at the floor, trying to imagine Colonel Murphy loving someone.

"I mean how much money can you give them? A solatium payment's not supposed to be a restitution for them, but a token of condolence and concern. But you can't make restitution for a dead boy."

38

Mason nods. Who's Murphy trying to convince? he thinks. Himself, for Christ's sake?

"They never saw that much money in their whole lives."

"That's something, Sir."

"Yeah, that's something." The Colonel tilts forward on his chair and puts his elbows on the desk. "It's funny, though, the way they were in here. The father kept asking General Lemming questions about *his* kids. Both he and the mother were in perfect control of themselves. They seem to have kind of a hardness about it all."

"I suppose you learn to accept it after a few years—or perhaps even expect it. I mean, eventually, we keep this up, and the VC keep it up, everybody's gonna get it, or at least be related to somebody who gets it."

"War's a dirty business, Mason. You know what Napoleon said, 'War is hell.' "

"I think it was Sherman said that, Sir."

"Oh, yeah, Sherman. I wish I could remember names like you can." He grinds out a cigarette. "What time is it?"

"1015, Sir."

"1015! Jesus, I was supposed to be at Third Brigade ten minutes ago! Have Kowalski get my chopper up here. You get wrapped up in stuff like this and you almost forget there's a goddam war going on.

"Kowalski, where's my chopper?"

★ 5 ★

The simplest and most relevant
statistical index of combat effec-
tiveness was thought to be the
average number of VC losses
(killed in action, prisoners of war,
and Hoi Chanh) inflicted daily by
the unit in question.—*Twelfth
Infantry Division Battle Analysis*

*Office of the Commanding General
Twelfth Infantry Division in Vietnam
1400 Hours, 12 March 1968*

TET had come and gone, leaving ineffaceable scars across South Vietnam and its people.

On the first morning of the offensive, a lieutenant had flown in from Free World Pad in Saigon, and leaping out of the chopper at Division had shouted, "Jesus Christ, they're even in the Embassy!" Well, in the Embassy garden, at any rate. This was the most visible and embarrassing of the enemy moves, but the others were much more significant, much worse. There was fighting in the streets up in Nha Trang; Da Nang had taken serious casualties from rocket and mortar attacks. For a while the Delta was quite literally on fire, the VC having gone after its major cities and the Americans having gone in after them: Can Tho, My Tho, Ben Tre, Vinh Long—cities of the relative stature of, say, Phoenix and Hartford and Madison and Lincoln. The attack was massive, astonishingly well coordinated, and for a while—it seemed—successful. Then it ran out of steam. The enemy was punished and he suffered grievously.

There was no Hué in the Delta, but the fighting subsided slowly enough. As Maye had suggested to General Lemming, the TET offensive did in retrospect stand comparison with the Battle of the Bulge. It had lost its momentum without having achieved what in March 1968 appeared to be its major goal: sufficient dislocation of morale in the United States to change the American war strategy. So it was thought then. The President's speech ("I do not wish to run again") was still three weeks in the future.

It seemed to General Lemming that the TET offensive had come close to another goal. One of his staff officers, writing an analysis for him, had put that objective in these words:

> Apparently shunning the slower, less immediately remunerative processes of political indoctrination and random employment of terror, the enemy employed the desperate expedient of coordinated, widespread terrorism. If he could not enlist the active support of the Vietnamese people to his cause, he could certainly disabuse them of any remaining pro-government bias. To do this he had only to demonstrate the inability of GVN (the Government of the Republic of South Vietnam) to protect the people it claimed to govern. He therefore launched a coordinated offensive of which the main targets were the major cities of South Vietnam.

The Twelfth Division had fought well. Colonel

Murphy, talking to the reporters, had not exaggerated his statistics, but the enemy offensive *had*, in Lemming's words, "impacted in the States," and a strange complex chemistry, devised jointly in Washington and Saigon, was mixing a new antidote. If cities had to be destroyed to save them during the allied counteroffensive the prognosis was hopelessly bad. Therefore the "allies" must return to the business of isolating and destroying large enemy units. Perhaps that would be "immediately remunerative."

On the morning of 11 March Lemming had attended a formal briefing at *his* commander's headquarters. General Rockacre had issued a new campaign directive, based on orders from his superiors. The relevant paragraphs were:

(1) The recent enemy counteroffensive has been thrown back everywhere, and the success of American units in-country has written a new page of gallantry in the annals of the Republic. It is imperative, however, that the follow-on operations by units assigned this command retain their momentum. Notwithstanding staggering losses, the enemy continues operations designed to cause terror among the people of South Vietnam . . .

(4) It is now apparent that our operations must aim at isolating, fixing, and destroying main-force NVA and VC units of battalion-size and larger *before* they are again able to threaten or infiltrate major population centers and force our units to conduct operations in these cities.

(5) It is therefore directed that you undertake operations in furtherance of *this* objective. The immediate criterion for judging their success will be reported numbers of enemy KHA (by body-count) . . .

(6) Allocations of supporting airmobile resources (AHC) will continue to be made among Divisions of this com-

mand on the basis of sound intelligence input and preliminary planning by each Division . . .

The directive struck the General—as he told his staff —as "meat and potatoes." "We are an *infantry* division. We are not configured, either as to attitude or TO & E, to do anything but locate VC and kill them off."

At the appointed time Colonel George Robertson, Lemming's First Brigade Commander, Lieutenant Colonel Chris Grubb, the Division G-3 (Operations Officer), and Lieutenant Colonel Frank Crauford, the G-2 (Intelligence Officer), join the General and the Chief of Staff in Lemming's office. To Robertson the invitation list is richly suggestive: he is the only commander present at a meeting of the efficient cabinet and it is obvious to him that there will be a venting of spleen. The other two brigade commanders, who were not summoned, are by temperament and success (the body-count criterion) much closer to Lemming than he is.

The General lights a cigarette and begins: "George, you were here for the briefing this morning. Does our intelligence brief for your AO jive with what your people tell you?" Lemming's eyes narrow and fasten on him like limpets.

"Yes, Sir, more or less. But of course briefings like these are out of date even before they're given. We have reasonable intelligence estimates, strong inputs every day. But we can't always capitalize on them."

Lemming, nastily: "Why not?"

Robertson says nothing for a few seconds, pretending to examine his fingernails. One of the staff lieutenant colonels coughs. "Because a boat goes ten knots and a chopper goes 120. You want the First Brigade to make good contacts, General—with all respect—you see to it that we get airmobile assets."

"We've been through this before, Robertson."

"Yes, Sir, we've been through this before, and the Brigade continues to get shortchanged."

"Crauford, here, says your intelligence is fragmentary, that your S-3 spends all his time on the ship watching movies."

"That's nonsense, General," Robertson rejoins, glaring at Crauford. "Dormeyer's the best Brigade '2' in Vietnam. He hasn't seen a movie since the Great Train Robbery."

Lemming looks over at Crauford. "Frank, tell Colonel Robertson what you heard from that Hoi Chanh the LRRP's brought in this morning."

"Sir. This guy rallied last night and claims to be part of the 317th Main Force battalion. He gave us an OB on them as complete as any I've ever heard. Thorough, detailed. It fits perfectly with what we know about the battalion: weapons, commanders, organization. The location he gives is more than plausible: it's been corroborated by agent-reports and SLAR read-outs . . ."

Robertson interrupts: "That would be . . . ?"

"That would be, Colonel, in the immediate vicinity of the juncture of the Giao Thong and the Rach Ba Nho, five clicks south of the My Tho, maybe twelve clicks from Cao Bai. The 317th moved there after TET.

It's been holed up there, apparently, for a month. We put their strength at 520."

"Weapons?"

"Very heavy. 82's. Maybe a couple of 120's. 3.5's. 75 Recoillesses. B-40's. They could raise hell with the tango boats."

Lemming hasn't taken his eyes off Robertson during this exchange. Now he leans forward over the coffee table and looks at his mapboard, on which has been taped a 1:50,000 map of central Kien Hoa Province. He props the mapboard up on his knees so the others can see it, at the same time studying the area Crauford has targeted. He hammers at the place with his forefinger. "That's where they are, Robertson, in there. And they're not gonna stay in there. Where's your anchorage?"

"Sa Dec."

"Could you launch from there?"

"No, Sir. Too far. We'd have to displace the MRB, anchor off Thoi Son, and launch from there. All of which assumes you can break loose the choppers you've scheduled all next week for the 2nd and 3rd Brigades. I'm not going in there straight riverine."

"Robertson, you'll go in there on your *feet*, if you have to . . ."

"Even though I can't walk on water."

The irreverence is a mistake. No one laughs.

"On your goddamn feet, if I say so." Lemming eases up quickly. "I can get you a helicopter company for a day, maybe two."

"It would help," Robertson says, fingering the map. "We've been down that river before, you remember. We lost our lead tango boat and most of the platoon on it. It's three miles of solid ambush-site. If I can airlift in a company, say, an hour before the riverine convoy goes in, I can draw the ambushes away from the banks, make them think the whole brigade's coming in airmobile from the south. Then . . ."

Lemming breaks in. "Good. Look alright to you, Grubb? Crauford? Murphy?" He smiles familiarly at his staff people. You gentlemen excuse yourselves now. I want to talk to Colonel Robertson. He'll get back to you later, maybe tomorrow."

The staff officers get up, salute woodenly, and leave.

Colonel Robertson, angry and depressed and his face showing it, waits for the controlled explosion, a performance he knows will be as carefully orchestrated as any battle the Twelfth Division has fought during Lemming's time as Commanding General. He is a huge bluff man, this Robertson, a man Lemming has disliked from their first meeting, and for whom the General's hatred seems to grow by the day.

Mercifully, Lemming is direct with him: "Who's Antony, no, *Anthony* Trollope?" He holds up a small Everyman's Library edition of *The Prime Minister*. "My aide gave me this at lunch. It's got your name in it. He says it fell out of your pocket at the helipad this morning."

46

"British novelist, General. You'd like him."

"You read this stuff in the chopper?"

"Yes, Sir. Flying point-to-point. Why not?"

Lemming ignores the question. "George, you've had the 1st Brigade three months and you haven't done a fucking thing with it." It scans well, the way he says it, slowly and in cadence, not dropping the g. It is the educated man's way of being direct without sounding crude. "Not a fucking thing."

The Brigade Commander does not answer. Instead he studies the toys on the General's desk. Lemming, his voice cold and without tone, continues:

"IV Corps below the River is lousy with VC. The MRB gets mortared two nights out of three. Your body-count is a standing joke. Tell you what, Robertson, you have one week to produce. Two full-strength battalions that lie in those goddamn boats and watch movies and stuff their faces all day. Get them off the boats and into the goddamn field. Do I make myself . . ."

"Yes, General, quite clear."

Lemming stares deliberately at the wet half-circles below the underarms of Robertson's fatigue jacket and finishes up calmly: "Don't hand me a ration of shit, George. Just get out of here."

The most effective dressing-downs are always quietly delivered, and Lemming has never raised his voice during the interview. Colonel Robertson knows—it is as simple as this—that he will be relieved unless he achieves a good body-count based on a major contact, and though he hates Lemming he knows the General can ruin him, can keep him from being a general, can keep him from riding through Persepolis, can make it difficult for him to keep paying his son's tuition at Cornell, can keep him from commanding a division himself some day, can vindicate his own wife's hatred for what he has been doing with his professional life, can make him a retired colonel selling fire insurance, with a Legion of Merit in his buttonhole. Can ruin him. The prospect is discomfiting even to George Robertson.

How superb, he thinks, to have reached over the desk, over the ludicrous, self-advertising bibelots, to have grabbed this paunchy creature by the lapels of his jungle fatigues and shake him until the blood drained from his face. He does none of these things, of course, only runs his tongue over his lips and nods in assent. "Yes, Sir." And he can't help reflecting, as he walks out the door, that in two weeks—perhaps in a week—Lemming will be decorating him and joining him to make the rounds of the wounded in the forward hospital, saying, "Goddamit, Robertson, you get that brigade cranked up good and proper and it fights damn well. Now keep it up . . ."

Thus he leaves Division headquarters for the drive to the helipad and the short flight out to the Samson, his command ship, anchored thirty miles up-river. Once more unto the breach, misfit, he thinks, smiling at the office personnel as he passes them.

What a waste.

48

✶ 6 ✶

THERE are not many like Robertson commanding brigades in Vietnam; he is anything but the Twelfth Infantry Division *beau ideal*. He certainly does not qualify as a "real sharp individual," as "aggressive," as a "hard-charger," and his image is only accentuated by his nickname—Shuffling George. He is loved by his staff; tolerated by the other two brigade commanders and light colonels on Lemming's staff, none of whom sees him as a threat; despised by Lemming and the ADC's.

Robertson has come by his brigade in Vietnam—his only major combat command—by a route that those who do not like him are disposed, if they are in a good humor, to call circuitous. He has all the wrong "tickets" and has long since been written off as a man whose colonelcy will be terminal.

The Pomfret School yearbook for 1946 noted that eight of that June's graduates were bound for New Haven, Connecticut; five for Harvard; three for Charlottesville; others for Williams, Penn, Haverford,

Stanford—and one, George Robertson, for the "West Point Military Academy." That he should have chosen West Point was thoroughly in keeping with what was known of him at the time—that he was unsettled, literary, overweight, insouciant—so why the hell not? His father supposed it might be a panacea: George would be straightened out; few of his business associates knew West Point was free. There was a Rogers Peet ad in a West Point alumni magazine he'd once seen in a dentist's office; George would have to serve only two or three years after his commissioning. To his mother the idea of Georgie-Porgie at West Point seemed deliciously absurd. This shaggy female, whose pleasant habit it was to drink gin-rickeys at 9 A.M. on weekend mornings and snore through sermons at the First Congregational Church in Lenox, was utterly unconcerned.

George's arrival at West Point in July 1946 began his alienation from the American military, a progressive disaffection from its ethic, its society, its habits of mind. On the sweltering morning he first passed under the sally-port he was instantly accosted by the first upperclassman to see him: "Drag in that slimy chin, Mister," he was told. George imagined the 4711 on his face had not yet dried and brushed the back of his hand across the offensive spot. This seemed not to please the older cadet, who then told him to "suck in that fat gut." Whereupon George put out his hand to the other and told him to "cut the bullshit and give me the real dope on this place."

An inauspicious start. Similar jarring incidents followed in rapid succession. Told that his gray trousers were too long, George shortened them with a pair of pinking shears and wore them to a formal inspection, jagged edges, dangling threads, and all. Two weeks later, unable to open the bolt of his M-1 at an inspection by a brigadier general, he slammed the offensive instrument to the pavement, butt down, kicking the bolt home with his heel. His wiseacre roommates had put a box of Trojans in the chamber, and these were ejected as he kicked the bolt, bouncing off the leg of the Brigadier's aide.

For these and similar breaches of taste George spent most of his time in confinement. But the enforced restriction to his books seemed to avail little. In a class of 506 he was ranked 501 after his first year. He particularly despised mathematics, then (as now) regarded as a staple in the cadets' academic diet, a means to "inculcate rigor" in their thinking. He found satisfying corroboration for this particular dislike in his omnivorous, patternless reading. The bizzare Chindit commander Orde Wingate, for example, standing naked in his headquarters listening to Bach on a Gramophone —the denial, George imagined, of all "rigor," but a soldier of vision and imagination and flair. Churchill's *A Roving Commission* granted rigorous thinkers a perfect right to exist, so long as the right was not exercised around the author, and referred to algebraic symbols as "comical hieroglyphs." Didn't Churchill boast that he could not add fractions and whole numbers? . . . Thomas Wolfe, *The Green Hat*, Swinburne, Proust (whom he was discovered reading in a yearling calculus section), Scott Fitzgerald . . . George liked books.

Of course he was regarded as a poseur, for aesthetes

have never been in fashion at West Point. There were the clichés about Poe and Whistler . . . but had not some men made it through untouched by the order, the regularity, the precision, the "rigor"?

George would. He wrote verse, slept through reveille, executed truly inspired practical jokes, and came eventually to earn the puzzled respect of the more discerning of his classmates and instructors. Toward the end of his cadetship he refused the sergeant's stripe he was offered as a first-classman, said he wanted no such responsibility that was a fraudulent responsibility ("Has every man in your squad received his box-lunch for the train ride to Philadelphia?" "Jones's hair wants cutting." "Has Griffin turned in his rifle to have its firing-pin inserted?").

So George Robertson shuffled along, thinking himself a young Suvorov. Shuffled through dancing lessons, through Military Law, through Combat in Cities, through a hundred dress parades, and finally shuffled onto the platform in June 1950, where George Catlett Marshall handed him his diploma and commission in the Regular Army.

Three weeks later a telegram from the War Department reached him at Sea Island, Georgia, where he was spending his graduation leave, and two months after that he was in Korea. Here he established the reputation that would carry him along comfortably for the next eighteen years. His personality changed little, and Korea was a good war to be phlegmatic in. On one occasion his platoon was the only unit in its battalion to hold its position during a vicious Chinese night attack. "We spent too much time on these bunkers to leave them now," he explained later. In the morning, after a battalion counterattack had re-established the previous line, they found enemy soldiers stacked up like cordwood in front of his platoon's position. Robertson was given the DSC and told to cut his hair before reporting to Division for a new assignment.

After Korea his career veered off in irregular directions: the University of Madrid for a degree in Spanish (during this tour he met his wife, who was spending her junior year at Lake Erie College abroad); teaching Spanish at West Point; duty as a translator in Washington; two tours at the Embassy in Madrid. It was during the second of these that he was brought back into the fold and assigned to Vietnam. An old friend, a patron, was at USARV as G-1: a friend with a Robertsonian sense of humor. He got George assigned to Lemming's Division. "You two'll be good for each other," he said. Neither George nor the General would see the humor in the assignment. And now it had come down to this: either Shuffling George gave Lemming a large victory (that is, a good body-count) or he got relieved.

Why do people like Robertson stay in the Army?

For the hell of it.

★ 7 ★

THE organization of combat units in the Army is relentlessly triadic: three infantry brigades in an infantry division; three infantry battalions in a brigade; three rifle companies in a battalion; three rifle platoons in a company; three rifle squads in a platoon. There are local variations, of course, adaptations to tactical necessity. But not many.

Three infantry brigade commanders thus answered to General Lemming. Colonel Robertson, that complicated, flippant bear of a man, we have already met; by way of contrast something must be said of the colonels commanding the other two brigades.

Both were known throughout the Army as "Lemming people"; sometimes, maliciously and simply, as Lemmings. The professional world runs on patronage; the professional army—the "Old Army"—was and is no different. "That's George Lemming's fair-haired boy," men would say, watching an officer's career develop, regarding his ticket-punching progress through the accommodating military bureaucracy. They imagined

George Lemming had a hand in where the officer was sent, how his career matured, how rapidly he was promoted. It gave the cub a certain amount of clout to be known this way. And in his infrequent discomfitures lay veiled implicit threats: "You keep fucking with me and George Lemming will hear about it." Two such fair-haired boys—in truth one was forty-one, the other forty-four—Caspar Manley and Johnny Morton, were now commanding Lemming's 2nd and 3rd Brigades.

The General had known them both since Korea, where they had been lieutenants in his battalion. Two adjectives regularly appeared in their efficiency reports: "hard-charging" and "aggressive." Both were nothing if not aggressive: aggressive in combat, aggressive in conversation—when men talked to them they stood with their hands on their hips and put their faces six inches from theirs, trying to wilt them with their stares —aggressive in bearing, aggressive in seeking new responsibility, aggressive in the barber shop ("Take it all off, muy pronto!"), aggressive in working on their paratrooper boots, aggressive in studying field manuals (Manley read in a field manual every night before going to sleep and called himself to account in the morning for what he had read), aggressive in committing adultery on leave from combat, aggressive in aggrandizing decorations ("One more of these oak leaf clusters on your chest and you'll keel over, Johnny. No, seriously, I'm very proud of ya.")

In Manley, Lemming saw himself as he liked to think of himself fifteen years ago: bold, confident, again aggressive, stylishly flamboyant, tactically brilliant. Above all things, he valued Manley's possession of instinct, a certain military trait of character which manifested itself on the field of honor, a kind of sixth sense that told him where the VC were. On this instinct, which, though not unerring, was more frequently vindicated than proved wrong, Manley could build a battle, could "orchestrate forces" better than any commander in Vietnam. His casualties were quite heavy—indeed a cynical reporter once called him a "butcher"—but his body-count for two months running had been the highest for a unit its size in the whole combat theater. It was gratifying to the General to have such a commander working for him, a commander, moreover, whose instinct for elevation to brigadier matched his instinct for the whereabouts of the elusive enemy.

If Manley had any fault at all in Lemming's eyes, it was only this: he had no idea how to pace himself. After two or three long operations (perhaps two weeks of combat) he was often on the verge of total physical breakdown. At these embarrassing times the General would arrange for him to take two or three days' unofficial leave in Saigon, where he could sleep, get laid, and kill off a bottle or two of Jack Daniels. Two other things: Manley followed his orders with a proper mixture of care and imagination. And he never handed Lemming any shit.

The General liked to boast that Colonel Manley's unit—the 2nd Brigade—was his "brass section," a richly talented section of carefully chosen players immediately responsive to the will of their conductor-in-chief (Lemming). George Szell raises an eyebrow, crooks the little finger of his left hand, and the morning's enemy body-count soars to 150. Bravo! The response was invariably *fortissimo*. Again, an abrupt nod from the podium, the confident whimsy drains from the conductor's face, and another 200 slopes perish in a *Götterdämerung*.

Yet even great conductors sometimes forget their scores, or must concentrate on their string sections. When this happened to Lemming, Manley's brass could be counted on to play its part nicely—supplying a satisfactory *continuo* or an ungrudging *rubato*. "Hold your people back for a couple of days, Manley, I'm giving your helicopter assets to the 1st Brigade . . ." And the trumpets and horns and trombones played on confidently.

In truth the directive Lemming had received from II Field Force was only a redundancy for Manley's players: they had been "isolating, fixing, and destroying main-force VC units" with perfect success for months.

Morton was something of a plodder by comparison, a competent second-chair horn player next to a Dennis Brain. His instincts were professionalized to the point that his sensing of the enemy situation was occasionally dull and his tactics only workmanlike. But he had good men working for him, taut young battalion commanders, all of them very aggressive, and these made the 3rd Brigade a going concern. Morton, perceiving the understanding between them and the General, did not often interfere in their operations. He trusted their judgments (as he had to) and got them what they needed to do their work: airmobile companies to enable their troops to "pile on" the hapless VC, chinooks to displace the 105 batteries to support their enterprises. Morton's saving grace, besides the bright battalion commanders, was that he projected the deferential eagerness Lemming cherished in a subordinate. He was not a troublemaker in any sense of the word; but he wasn't an ass-kisser either. He was competent and sound, the twenty-seventh man in an army in which twenty-six generals are awarded marshal's batons.

In another idiom: he was a Cocker Spaniel who never soiled the rug.

By the standards used to measure the performance of every other brigade in Vietnam—reported enemy body-count—his 3rd Brigade was a smashing success. Only next to Manley's did it suffer in comparison. And only once had the 3rd Brigade been in trouble. That was before Morton's tenure as commander, when one of its line companies, in an uncontrollable access of zeal, had taken to clipping the ears of their dead enemies. Aggressive enough, but not very professional.

Morton and Manley and their brigades shared responsibility for the Division's assigned area of responsibility north of the northern branch of the Vietnamese Mekong, a river known variously as the Tien Giang or the Song My Tho. They had done everything asked of them, done their jobs professionally and well. Lemming bragged about them—especially Manley—whenever he saw the other II Field Force Division commanders. By their own criteria for success he could well be smug.

As for his 1st Brigade, his "River Lions," well, he'd just as soon you'd not ask him about that.

TWO

Brigade

In some ways it was like the debate of a group of savages as to how to extract a screw from a piece of wood. Accustomed only to nails, they had made one effort to pull out the screw by main force, and now that it had failed they were using and devising methods of applying more force still, of obtaining more efficient pincers, of using levers and fulcrums so that more men could bring their strength to bear. They could hardly be blamed for not guessing that by rotating the screw it would have come out after the exertion of far less effort; it would be a notion so different from anything they had ever encountered that they would laugh at the man who suggested it.

C. S. FORESTER
The General

★ 8 ★

G-3 Office
Headquarters, Twelfth Infantry Division
1600 Hours, 12 March 1968

"YOU did a good job, Compella, I'd like to keep you up here for the whole war."

Compella thanks the Major and stands easy in front of his desk in the noisy office just off the DTOC.

"But they're cleaning out the Academy. Colonel Plowman's battalion got the shit shot out of it last week and the 1st Brigade needs one-one bravos. You and the others the Academy sent over here for temporary duty have to go down to Plowman's battalion."

"When?"

"This afternoon. Sixty people went down there this morning. Plowman's is one of the riverine battalions, living on the MRB. It's anchored 30 clicks from here. Fifteen minutes in a chopper."

"How do I get down there?"

"Get your stuff together and Sergeant Hendrix will

drive you over to the helipad. You can hitch a ride out with the mail or maybe on Colonel Robertson's C and C. He's still here. Hang around until something is going out to the MRB. You have time to go to the PX and get what you need. OK?"

"Yes, Sir. Thank you, Sir."

"We can get you back up here in six or eight months. Keep your head down and don't be a fucking hero."

"Yes, Sir."

Thus: down to brigade, down to battalion, down to a company, down to a platoon. And then, if you're not a fucking hero in a plastic bag, back up to Division. The imagery is not lost on PFC Compella.

The rotors beat up a terrific dust at the helipad. Compella throws his stuff onto Robertson's C and C ship and climbs aboard, Shuffling George amused at his efforts to manhandle his equipment. He straps himself in, wedged between two other soldiers Robertson has offered rides to, and the chopper lifts off, cants oddly forward, beats into the wind and out over the river.

The Spec Four sitting at his left regards him coolly, remarking the shiny new fatigues and Compella's pasty complexion.

"Where you headed?"

"First of the 71st."

The Spec Four looks at the buck sergeant sitting on his left and grins. The Sergeant shakes his head slowly from side to side and spits on the floor of the slick. "That's nice, real nice. How long you been in-country?" he shouts. It is noisy in the huey.

"Eleven days."

"Shit. I got eleven days til my DEROS."

Compella looks over at him steadily, apprehensively. The two veterans remember how they felt when they flew out to join the riverine force. One can be expansive, even charitable, with eleven days left in-country.

"It ain't bad. You a one-one bravo?"

"Yeah."

"Well. Stay off point. Stay off rice-dikes. Stay alert. When you're most tired, like coming back from a patrol, that's when you get it. Just when you think you got it made—back to the ship, shower, food—that's when you get it. Stay down when you're in the boats. You'll be alright."

Compella, shy and nervous, is uncertain how to reply, so he asks: "Dja ever get laid in-country?"

The veterans laugh. "Yeah, once or twice," says the Spec Four. "It's like anywhere else, you look for it, you'll get it."

"Whaddya give 'em?"

"Script. Maybe two, three dollars. Sometimes cigarettes. The slopes like Salems. Anything menthol. Newports. Don't go in bareback."

The buck sergeant throws back his head and snorts with laughter. "Tell us all about it, Sanders."

"Not too clean, huh?" Compella says.

The Sergeant laughs again. "No, not too clean. But don't lose any sleep over it. You won't get much exposure."

Colonel Robertson has taken off his earphones and hung them around his neck. He sticks his head out into the slipstream like a St. Bernard riding in a station wagon. The wind feels good, healing. Already he has discovered the humor in Lemming's grim warnings and advice to him, has forgotten the scorn and anger in his voice. Helicopter flights are a restorative for him. What a lovely country it is, he thinks. From 1500 feet the late afternoon sunlight appears to have broken through the higher clouds blown before the monsoon, slanting down in luminous slides of gold, marking out scattered patches of rice paddy, isolating and arranging them like peridots on dark satin, bright yellow-green and glistening. Far off, almost at the horizon, an azure haze suggests the sea, and beneath the helicopter following its course, the great tawny river uncoils, stretches out like some gorged reptile. Almost nothing seems to move below, save an occasional fleck of white defining itself into a tiny figure poling along near the riverbank. In the far distance Robertson makes out the ships of the Mobile Riverine Base, five of them, riding at anchor like toy boats. He reaches around and pats Compella on the knee, pointing out the ships with his left hand. "That's your new home, Son, right down there." Compella nods at him gratefully. Funny-looking colonel, he thinks. Fatigues fit lousy. Jowly face. Friendly. "It's a hell of a good place to come back to after three or four days in the boonies."

And yet he is not condescending. "Boonies" sounds right coming out of his mouth, not like an officer trying to sound like a PFC. Once at West Point, Cadet Robertson had heard a lecturer say that the "gulf between officer and enlisted person is broad and deep.

64

The men *expect* you to keep your distance." It was a vaccination that never took.

The chopper is finally almost directly over the MRB, and now it descends in a series of falling concentric rings, as if whirling down a tornado, leveling off finally for its final approach to the flight deck of the *Samson*. While it settles on its skids an officer runs out to meet Colonel Robertson, catches his mapboard, and walks with him off the flight deck.

As the Colonel gets to the head of the ladder leading to his stateroom below, he turns around suddenly and waves at Compella, who is wrestling again with his equipment.

"Where you going, Son, 1st of the 71st?"

"Yes, Sir."

"Well. Keep your head down. You'll see me again. That's a good battalion."

★ 9 ★

"Tell you what, Robertson, you have one
week to produce."—*George Lemming,
Major General, to George Robertson, Colonel, 12 March 1968.*

"And now beware of rashness; beware of
rashness, but with energy and sleepless vigi-
lance, go forward, and give us victories."—
*Abraham Lincoln to Joseph Hooker, Major
General, 26 January 1863.*

IT is like an order to take a crap. Defecate me bodies,
Robertson. Do it in one week. Sooner if possible. Do
it yesterday. In effect, it means Robertson must "produce" a "contact," a contact on which to build, about
which to orchestrate forces, on which to feed the
egos of the battalion commanders who love to orchestrate things. Find the VC and pile on. "You do it right,
George—I don't have to tell you this—and your companies can sweep the area the next morning and count
bodies. And negligible friendly casualties . . ."

(And before the TET offensive there had been the
great semantics war. "By the goddamn way, Robertson,
MACV has changed the fucking name: it is not search
and destroy any more. It is search and *clear,* or if your
plans officer is a wise-ass, 'reconnaissance-in-force'

66

is acceptable. Only stop sending my G-3 people OPLANS with 'search and destroy' written in as the mission. Clear?"

Quite clear, General. Do not destroy the enemy or the hamlets they occupy at night; clear them. See that clown down there in his sampan, the one riding low in the water? *Clear* him. Then clear your weapons. We don't want people hitching rides in choppers with their weapons not cleared. Clear? Clear. Robertson thinks of Danny Kaye: get in, get on with it, get it over with, and get out. Get it? Got it. Good.)

He lays his Trollope on the desk and considers. The Army insists on its euphemisms, its circumlocutions, its depersonalization of language. "You individuals over there," bellows the sergeant-major. "Get busy and utilize those entrenching tools." That is, "dig." "We've got some real sophisticated new hardware, Mr. Secretary; it facilitates our operations." "Caspar Manley orchestrates forces better than any brigade commander in Vietnam. His people really impact on the enemy."

The linguistic symphonies all have their codas, too, their summations. They are heavily percussive, and the players are the rankers and the company-grade officers: "Zap that slope. Waste that gook. Use them up."

Robertson admired Lemming's immunity to all this. He used the straight words mostly. "There is no god-damn reason to pad body-counts. You get the contact, you make the kills.

"People notice these things, Robertson. You know the body-count charts we keep in the Lion's Den? (a small briefing-room just off Lemming's office). The

Field Force commander comes in here once or twice a month and looks them over, and he sees 2nd Brigade: 4100 KIA, by BC; 3rd Brigade: 3100 KIA, by BC. And then he looks at your brigade's figure and he says, 'Who commands your 1st Brigade, General Lemming?' I tell him, and he nods, not saying anything—yet. It doesn't look very good."

The man's got a voracious appetite, Robertson reflects.

Robertson fights his brigade in the central Mekong Delta, south of the Song My Tho, the main west-east branch of the Mekong system, a deep turgid river almost as wide as the Hudson at the Tappan Zee; sometimes along the Song Ba Lai, sometimes in the Rung Sat Special Zone; sometimes south of Sa Dec; sometimes in Kien Hoa Province; on occasion even as far south as the U Minh forest. Wherever the rivers are deep enough to sail his brigade into wherever his intelligence people think there may be VC, he fights his brigade. He goes to each new battleground slowly, too, but more of that later.

With that unexpected and engaging aptitude of his for serious music, George Lemming once shocked Robertson by an allusion to the Mekong as an "Asian *Moldau*." Robertson was impressed. The simile is not inexact: somewhere in the Himalayan headlands the stream springs to life, clear and fast-running, making its way south, nourished by the brooks of the virid Thai and Lao hills. It gathers to stature hundreds of miles above the dusky Cambodian capital, becoming a quiet determined flood too great for two riverbanks to contain. Above the Vietnamese border it splits apart, the offspring generally pushing south by southeast, overrunning and enriching the great Delta below Saigon Men give the branches of the Vietnamese Mekong the general name of the "Mekong distributary." These grow eventually to rivers as wide and majestic as the Cambodian Mekong itself.

In effect, they make three great triangular islands of the central Delta, islands in turn penetrated and cross-sected by lesser streams and canals, creating the "characteristic riverine environment" the Field Manuals speak of, a mysterious alien land of ricepaddy and jungle.

It is the home of perhaps seven millions, of whom twenty-five thousand arrest the unswerving attention of George Lemming and the fitful prodded curiosity of his brigade commander. These are the Delta VC, wily creatures, forms of human life every Lemming acidly characterizes as "slopes," poor deluded bastards somehow infected with a strangely sustaining but altogether toxic virus called the dialectic, a dialectic worked out by another fool last century in the British Museum. ("You agree, General Lemming?" "Well, I don't know: I suppose that's true in a somewhat fanciful way. They're not all communists, of course, but COSVN is, and they get their orders down through the COSVN chain-of-command. Don't glamorize these people into nationalists or freedom-fighters. They do what COSVN tells them, the ones we're really after. It all comes down to that.")

The VC Robertson and his men fight are organized in different ways. There are, first, the Main Force units, usually reinforced infantry battalions directly subordinate to COSVN or to Regional Headquarters, units as lean and hard and professional as anything Fort Benning ever dreamed of. They comprise three or four companies, plus headquarters elements, five or six hundred men in the whole battalion. Funny how easily they get around, without LST's and APB's and hueys, how they can disappear like pieces of riverbank collapsing into the flood, how suddenly they can be six hundred men concentrated in superbly fortified and camouflaged positions along the riverbanks and in the woodlines.

Robertson's people also fight units directly under Provincial or District Party Committees, not as good as the Main Force battalions but dangerous and elusive enough, armed well enough to raise hell with the Americans. And they fight the plain old ordinary guerrillas, the part-time soldiers, the ones that blow up orphanages and offer the troops Pepsi with glass dust in the bottles. ("Dirty things like that, right, General Lemming?" "Yes, more or less. The Main Force units are quite professional . . .")

Shuffling George gets to grips with these enemy in strange ways. After a fashion, he is in command of an outfit called the Mobile Riverine Force. The Force moves, after a fashion, to landing sites from which its infantry can maneuver to where Robertson's staff think the VC are hiding. After a fashion, the VC change their hiding places. Sometimes the 1st Brigade discovers these retreats, and the VC pay a certain price—provided all their escape routes are blocked. Often, however, the VC get loose, make good their escape, and the results are "inconclusive." Often again, especially in the rainy season (April to October in the Delta), Robertson's troops make no contact at all. They are put ashore only to stagger around in the swamps and paddies until 20 or 30 percent have foot diseases. Then they return to their ships and watch movies and read skin books while their feet recuperate. After the "no contact" operations the Brigade Plans Officer sends forward combat-after-action reports which insist, on the contrary, that the operation *was* at least something of a success, *viz:* ". . . further, elements of the Riverine Force destroyed twenty-seven (27) enemy bunkers, captured twenty pounds of documents, and a small cache of medical supplies."

Think of Primo Carnera going after Willie Pep in a pigsty ten miles square.

Virginia Mayo and Laurence Harvey are in the wardroom tonight aboard the *Samson,* the Force's command ship riding at anchor off the city of Sa Dec. The junior officers are absorbed in the siege of Acre. Miss Mayo is being hypnotized by a Moor with a moonstone. Topside in his stateroom, his dressing-down having done nothing visible to stir him up, Robertson is already in bed reading *The Way We Live Now.*

For even if he could communicate Lemming's deadly earnestness to his staff, his ultimatum to the 1st Brigade, there is little he can do to conjure up a VC Main Force battalion for him. Three decks down in the *Samson,* Robertson's S-2, a major called Pearl Dormeyer, is evaluating enemy information with his usual plodding thoroughness: intelligence bulletins from Division, aerial photos, reports from friendly Vietnamese agents, SLAR read-outs. He and the S-3 have talked briefly with the Colonel on the latter's return from Division, but their work can hardly be speeded. Robertson reads his novel with a clear conscience.

In truth the Riverine Force of which his 1st Brigade was the infantry element had outlived its tactical usefulness. The VC had grown wise to its ways, its cumbersome flailing reactions to their changing dispositions, its pathetic feints and countermovements. During the TET counteroffensive it had enjoyed a certain recrudescence of its early glamor, had even, in the words of COMUSMACV, "saved the Delta." But already its ability to gain and hold contact with the enemy had again diminished sharply. There is no doubt General Lemming understood that the Brigade's problem had little to do with George Robertson. The Riverine Force simply wasn't, as he told a Washington *Post* reporter, "properly configured for this kind of war."

No one in the Mobile Riverine Force seemed to know how the outfit had come into existence. Rumors circulated: it was a device to get the Navy into Vietnam in a large way, closer than the range of the heavy lenses on the bridge of a Seventh Fleet cruiser. Contrariwise—more convincingly—it was devised as a means to solve the overwhelming problem posed by the Delta as a military arena—poor mobility.

Calculate the depths of the major branches of the southern Mekong. Can they float capital ships? Or at least major ships of the amphibious Navy, LST's and the like? It was determined they were deep enough for LST's and ships of comparable draft, and that ships of this type could be fitted out to carry large numbers of infantry and their combat support elements and equipment. Four or five such ships could house a brigade-minus, two battalions reinforced: eighteen hundred soldiers. Together these ships could make a floating base of operations, almost wholly self-sustaining and capable of sailing at will almost anywhere in the Delta.

They could get the infantry close to hostile positions, but not quite close enough. Since troop-carrying helicopters were at a premium in the spring of 1966, and since even small flattops were too deep of draft to navigate the rivers, it was decided to refit the old Mike-6's, which had carried the Marines ashore in the Pacific in World War II, for similar service in Vietnam. Converted, the Mike-6 hulls were developed into ATC's (armored troop carriers—called tango boats by the troops), CCB's (Command and Communications boats), and "Monitors." These and similar vessels could navigate the canals and smaller streams of the Delta. They were heavily armed and armored: all with gun turrets aft mounting .50-caliber machine guns and MK-18 grenade launchers and belt-fed 20mm cannon. The monitors also had turrets forward with another .50 machine gun and 40mm cannon; sometimes they even carried 81mm mortar tubes mounted amidships.

The ATC's each could carry an infantry platoon. A

few were specially fitted out for support missions. Some, for example, mounted their own tiny flight decks capable of landing helicopters; others were developed as forward hospitals or resupply vessels; yet another carried a tank of liquid napalm and was used as a flame-thrower. With a fine sense of nonchalance men called it a "zippo."

The theorists, having solved the problem of tactical mobility in the Delta, looked around for troops to enjoy this immunity from the "tyranny of terrain." It was a logical mission for the Marine Corps, but the marine infantry was committed elsewhere, up in I Corps.

Now it happened that at about this time (in mid-1966) the Twelfth Infantry Division was also being prepared for Vietnam duty, tentatively in the Delta. The joint planners decided that the redoubtable Lionheads should be tasked with the infantry mission of the Riverine Force; the Division should designate one of its brigades as the Force's infantry element and place it on a semi-detached status for service with the Navy in the Delta. The 1st Brigade was chosen. All of this was done some time before either Lemming or Robertson was assigned to the Twelfth Division. With the clairvoyance of hindsight, Lemming often asserted that such a transfer of the Division's strength from the immediate will of its commander would have been made over his dead body, and that the whole concept was, in his favorite word of contempt, lousy.

"A boat is too goddamn slow," he would say. And to discomfit the distinguished Defense Department visitors who frequently came to the Division, wanting only to fly down and see the Mobile Riverine Force, he had had an in-house cost-effectiveness expert prepare figures to show that the Force was not nearly so able to "capitalize on lucrative targets" as a single airmobile battalion might have been.

However, the Force was in existence when he came to the Lionheads, and Commander Naval Forces Vietnam was very proud of it. Nominally this functionary and Lemming shared joint control of the Force. In fact, it was largely independent of the control of anyone. There was some doubt, even, as to which embarked commander—the Army Brigade Commander or the Navy Task Force Commander (a Captain, whom his staff called "Commodore") was really the senior authority. In the directive which initially prescribed command relationships theirs was to be one of "co-operation and coordination." It was a hedging, equivocal arrangement, entirely at the mercy of those assigned to the two jobs. Disagreements as to strategy and tactics were resolved by compromise, which kept all concerned quite happy, especially the VC.

In truth, the two services got along quite well together. The Army officers thought their naval counterparts a bit stuffy: they were resentful that the naval officers weren't in the field as much as they should be, that they were too eager to enforce the wooden protocol of the wardroom and the mess, too inclined to "overstaff"—to appoint to counterpart staff positions officers somewhat senior to their infantry comrades-in-arms. But the problems weren't serious. The food was good, the ships were air-conditioned, and their stores nicely stocked. And most of the Navy knew their business.

In theory the nature of the Force's operations was simple enough. Two reinforced battalions would be embarked on the amphibious ships, the whole then sailing to anchorages from which it could launch strike operations into the interior Delta. The infantry battalions would disembark, load the ATC's, and proceed in riverine convoy to preselected "beaches" where they would go ashore and try to get a grip on the VC. The ATC's and other boats would then perform support missions: establishing blocks, resupplying the troops, providing fire support. For the infantry the object, generally, was to pin the VC up against some stream sealed off by the boats.

Artillery would be made water-mobile too, the 105 batteries mounted on barges which could accompany the rest of the riverine convoys to positions from which they could offer support for the infantry. The 105's and the Monitors could provide sufficient fire support for the infantry, combining to "prep" the "beaches" just as huey gunships prepped LZ's elsewhere. There were other sources of fire support available: air strikes by USAF jets, 155 batteries, the zippo boat.

A characteristic operational sequence might go something like this: the Brigade S-2, Major Dormeyer, working with his Navy staff counterpart, would process enemy intelligence from available sources. Together they would estimate the whereabouts and strengths of enemy units, presenting target options to the operations and plans officers of both services. These officers would then assign priorities to the targets and draw up operations plans for getting at them—schemes of landing and maneuver and fire support. Perhaps two days before an operation was to be launched the planners would present their schemes to the Brigade Commander and the Commodore, making informed guesses that the targeted enemy units would stay where they had been identified, or that their movements would be the expected ones.

Once these two—Robertson and Captain Jacobs, USN—agreed on the target and plan, serious preparations got under way. Calls would go out for supporting aid and airmobile assets. Clearances for fires would be obtained from District Chiefs of the unhappy areas into which the infantry was to be "inserted." Ammunition, food, water, maps, etc., were given the infantry battalions, and elaborate formal briefings were presented their commanders. Tides were carefully calculated so that there would be no embarrassments involving ATC's run aground. Departure times for the different riverine craft were selected.

Let us say an element of a VC Provincial Mobile Battalion has been reported refitting 100 kilometers from the current anchorage of the Mobile Riverine Base (MRB). All preparations having been made, the infantry companies would line up on the AMMI pontoons locked in place alongside the barracks ships, receive last-minute briefings, and board the ATC's. So that they could make their beach landings shortly after first-light, the ATC convoys would leave the Base anchorage at 0100. Meantime the artillery barges, being slower, would already have set out on their journey to their prospective fire bases.

An artillery beach preparation would be fired fifteen or twenty minutes before the boats dropped their ramps against the tangled thick vegetation of the riverbanks. The infantry would land and go about its business. At about the same time, the Mobile Riverine Base would weigh anchor and sail to a new anchorage as close as possible to the target area.

Two or three days later the troops would be "back-loaded" and return to the MRB.

There were severe tactical problems, most of them inescapable: it was, for example, unthinkable to put infantry ashore outside the "fans" of the barge artillery batteries, unless there were ARVN or other American land-based artillery already placed to support them. Therefore, since the artillery barges had to be in place before the troops could land, it was easy for the VC to determine the general area of the landing by calculating a circle with a 9000-meter radius centered on the location of the barges—9000 meters being the effective range of the 105 artillery.

Further, the VC quickly learned the drafts and speeds of the ships and boats and took care to isolate themselves from streams broad and deep enough to float them.

Also, the Mobile Riverine Base had to be protected. This dissipated the strength of one of the embarked infantry battalions by at least 25 percent; likewise, the barge artillery needed infantry protection.

And at any time 10 or 15 percent of the infantry might be on R and R or laid up with foot diseases.

Last, the Twelfth Division competed for airmobile companies (abbreviated: AHC's—units of ten "slicks" each, the ten able to transport sixty troops in one "lift") with the other infantry divisions and independent brigades in II Field Force. The Division had to "prove" that it had a greater need for the AHC's than the others it competed with. To do this it had to demand the projected plans of its subordinate brigades several days in advance of their execution. For their part the brigades had to make as strong a case as possible for their right to the AHC's.

In Robertson's view it was a foolish system. It resulted in elaborate plans targeted on enemy units whose whereabouts by the time the AHC's were actually assigned could only be guessed at. In competing for the helicopter assets the brigades only benefited their real competitors, the VC. For it happened that the brigade whose colonel had the most clout with Lemming (usually Manley's), or whose operations officer was most persuasive, usually got the helicopters. In this competition the 1st Brigade made out badly. "After all," Crauford once told Robertson, "your transport is organic: you've got the boats."

And the Division staff came to expect Robertson's resignation to this invariable trump. His arguments, they knew, and he knew, were usually foredoomed.

Many years ago George Robertson had a black First Sergeant working for him, and he remembers him now as the finest soldier—officer, NCO, or private—he ever knew. On the 1st Sergeant's desk was a placard which read:

> God grant me the wisdom to know the things I can change, the grace to accept the things I can't change, and the sense to know the difference.

It is an old cliché, but it has served (as much as anything can serve) as Robertson's standard for a long time. He believes in it. It is why he is in bed now, reading Trollope.

★ 10 ★

U.S.S. *Samson, APB-58*
1800 Hours, 12 March 1968

TEN fattish little men, all the same man, appear in different poses in different brandy advertisements pasted on the bulkhead of the stateroom on the *Samson* inhabited by Major Charles R. ("Chick") Claiborn, the Operations Officer of the 1st Brigade (Riverine) of the Twelfth Infantry Division. Major Claiborn is the most military man in this story. "Jesus," said the clerks in Lemming's front office the day he reported at Division, "he marches even *indoors*." They overheard General Lemming and Colonel Murphy interviewing Claiborn that day, almost eight months ago now, and they hardly believed their ears. Neither did Lemming for that matter—though fortunately for the Major, he was in one of his more accommodating moods.

"I came to Vietnam this time for one reason, General: to get a battalion." "But you're a *major*," Colonel Murphy broke in, nonplussed. "We've got light colonels

81

in this headquarters begging for battalions. Are you on a promotion list?" Claiborn was not on a promotion list. "But I can command a battalion, and when the chance comes up, I want to be considered . . ."

The Courvoisier Brandy ads accompany Major Claiborn on all his assignments and are carefully stuck up on the walls wherever he lives. Bonaparte at the Adige. The First Consul rearing up on a horse—the St. Bernard. Napoleon at Austerlitz. Napoleon at Aspern. Above these martial poses, which Claiborn has cut from the pages of *The New Yorker* because of the quality of the paper, he always places two printed mottos: LET US NOT HEAR OF GENERALS WHO CONQUER WITHOUT BLOODSHED (Clausewitz), and FORTUNE FAVORS THE PREPARED MAN (Machiavelli). He keeps with him also—on the *Samson* as on all assignments—two cans of brasso, six of black kiwi, his four West Point yearbooks, a footlocker full of paperbacks on strategy and tactics and military history, a fishing-tackle box full of extra insignia, a gleaming new Olivetti Lettera 22—on which he types entries into his journal each night—and an incredible array of small arms fitted into shelves in a box constructed specially for them: a Russian PPSH-41 submachine gun (7.62 caliber, 71-round drum: "you can really talk to a crowd with this motherfucker"); a Mauser M-32 machine pistol (7.63: "the nice thing about this one is that it's got such a slow cyclic rate: they can feel each bullet going in; if you hold it sideways the crowd'll really listen"); an MP-44 Stürmgewehr (7. 92); and a Schmeisser submachine gun.

82

Claiborn loves these guns and he has used them all, saying "I can't look at a slope, or even think of one without seeing the crosshair of a weapons-sight on his forehead."

He loves war and yet is not perhaps a wholly bad man. He is responsive to the will of his superiors, efficient in executing their orders (with the exception that he will not send out body-count patrols during fire fights), and he is an incredibly brave leader of troops and a compassionate mentor to the men assigned his command. "He's the guy you want to be with when the shit hits the fan," they say of him. The members of the Robertson Riverine staff call him "Marvin Military," but they call him this banteringly, respectfully.

It is his second tour in Vietnam, the first having been spent as a Special Forces "A" team leader in 1965, up in II Corps. And it can now be added that he owns the distinction of being the only major in the Division to have commanded an infantry battalion—the assignment made unhesitatingly by General Lemming on the death of the battalion commander to whom Claiborn had originally been assigned as executive officer. Claiborn kept command of this battalion for two months, until the II Field Force commander pressured Lemming into replacing him with one of his own protégés, a senior lieutenant colonel just arrived in-country from the War College.

The public might wonder about this: why, if Claiborn was a decent battalion commander, was he removed from his post after only two months? Why not promote him to light colonel and let him keep it? Well, times have changed. It is no longer 1944 with Frank Lovejoy reaching into his footlocker, pulling out a tarnished old set of lieutenant colonel's leaves and pinning them on Dana Andrews' collar ("Here, Major, you've earned these") and Andrews, abashed ("What the . . . ?"). No. Promotion is now regularized, is almost wholly by seniority. Claiborn has made it to senior major as fast as possible. Still, he is but two years shy of the age at which Jim Gavin became a major general.

And perhaps it is just as well. The Major's battalion fought well but took terrible casualties. When a new lieutenant colonel reported in, Lemming decided to remove Claiborn from his battalion and send him to Robertson, hoping to invigorate the Riverine Brigade and at the same time to have a congenial tactical mind, a "Lemming man," on Robertson's staff. For few people thought better of Major Charles Claiborn than George Lemming.

Yet, unexpectedly, nobody came to think better of George Robertson than Charles Claiborn. Strange the way things work out like this in war. Shuffling George and the Major rapidly became fast friends and trusting comrades. It took Claiborn less than a week to diagnose the tactical problems of the Mobile Riverine Force and to understand that Robertson was doing the best he could under the circumstances. Once he had reached his conclusions he became a fiercely loyal subordinate. "What's wrong with the Riverine Force, Chick?" Robertson asked him one night, absently, expecting a conversational reply. To which his new Operations Officer replied: "Simple. The VC in the Delta will fight

84

us only on their terms or when we achieve tactical surprise. Several factors preclude our surprising them: security leaks—the LNO's clear our plans through ARVN; recon over the prospective TAOR's; airstrikes on the landing beaches—the VC see where the tango boats are going to put the troops ashore and clear the area; artillery preps on the beaches; insecure radio nets; the slowness of the ships; VC familiarity with the capabilities of the assault craft . . ."

Robertson was deeply impressed: the Major had been with him only three days. From that night forward his confidence in Claiborn was absolute. They complemented each other well: Robertson huge and slow, difficult, sloppy, seemingly unconcerned; Claiborn compact, self-assured, hard-driving, committed.

It was to Claiborn that Robertson turned as soon as he got back from Division. "Lemming's after us again, Charles. He wants a contact and a Ringling Brothers body-count and he wants it ASAP. You might go below and talk to Dormeyer and the plans officers and see if you can get a good fix on the 317th. They couldn't have crossed the river." Claiborn nodded sympathetically: "Yes, Sir. I'll get back to you in the morning."

The 317th Main Force battalion was an old nemesis. The riverine troopers spoke of it the same way the British in the desert talked of Rommel and the Afrika Corps. And yet they knew little of the unit because they had never really come to grips with it. They knew it had given three ARVN regiments bloody noses which had put each of them out of action for months. For almost two years—since the summer of 1966— it had been "sighted" (to use the S-2 euphemism for "hearing an unverified rumor about") fairly regularly in both Kien Hoa and Dinh Tuong provinces. During TET it had occupied and virtually eliminated the village of Thanh Nhoc, which the ARVN had been defending. A week later it had vanished.

Robertson, even before hearing Division's intelligence, assumed the 317th was still in Kien Hoa (a correct assumption, it will appear), but he was not sanguine about the possibility of surprising an enemy Main Force battalion on its home ground in a concentrated disposition. Kien Hoa, though not a large province, is big enough: about 830 square miles of mangrove, sugar cane, coconut groves, some open country, depressingly free of access streams capable of floating river assault craft. And the tributaries of the My Tho and Co Chien rivers which did snake their way out of Kien Hoa were invariably banked with foliage thick enough to blunt any artillery preparation and dense enough to make enemy exit almost undetectable.

Yet the 317th, if it could be pinpointed and fixed in position by a combination of river assault boats and helicopter-borne rifle companies, might turn and fight. The VC were rarely stupid enough to fight for terrain, or to "prove themselves" against American infantry, but Kien Hoa was a vital rear area of the VC Military Region II. It contained three known "secret zones" thought to conceal huge, carefully dispersed supply dumps where weapons and ammunition and rice had been secreted. To protect these the 317th might fight.

Kien Hoa is shaped like a jagged wedge. Its northern boundary is the My Tho River (the most northerly branch of the Mekong), its southeast limit the South China Sea; on the west and southwest it extends to the Song Co Chien. Like most Delta provinces it is thickly populated: the 1960 census reports 675,000 residents ("All of whom hate our fucking guts," Lemming once told Rockacre), the vast majority of them rice farmers. Already the trafficability—quite satisfactory in the dry season—was becoming questionable as the monsoon began to buffet and soak the land regularly. Again, Robertson reflected, the Brigade would be at the mercy of the "whims of God." If God made a river that happened to lead to an enemy position, or if He put it in the mind of Lemming to take Manley's helicopter assets away from him and give them to Robertson, the Commanding General's thirst for a big contact might be slaked. Otherwise—he chuckled to himself—well, he hadn't read *Orley Farm* yet.

Claiborn, as operations officer of the Army element of the Riverine Force, was not expected to be a planner. Nominally he supervised the plans shop, or rather its Army element: a captain, a first lieutenant, and three or four bright enlisted men. Sometimes he acted as liaison between them and the intelligence officers, who made the common assumption that a major was more worthy to be listened to than a captain. As a rule, however, he put in long hours in the field with Colonel Robertson, overseeing and coordinating the execution of the plans his people and their navy counterparts worked up. In the evenings, aboard ship, it was his habit to pour himself a neat bourbon, work on his guns, or read in professional journals: *Army, Armor,* the *Naval Institute Proceedings.* One wasn't supposed to drink on ship, but few people disturbed the Major in his stateroom. And, after all, what could a senior army officer say to an officer of Claiborn's reputation who—while most of the staff looked at movies in the wardroom—applied himself to the written theory and science of war?

For the officers of the Riverine Force, and for the troops as well, war seemed to be turned on and off like an electric light. The "field" was hell, but there was always—a day or two away—the blessed quiet and coolness of the ship, clean sheets, one's stereo equipment; cameras and novels. Claiborn reflected that he was like an F-86 pilot in the Korean War; one practiced one's profession, bit the bullet so to speak, got shot or did not get shot, and then returned to what might have been an American community with all the amenities but women.

Tonight, on leaving Robertson, he did not go to his stateroom. Instead he made his way through the wardroom, past the galley, along the antiseptically clean passageways of the *Samson,* down two ladders and finally to the Intelligence Shop to talk with Major Dormeyer and Commander Craig. He had carefully formulated the questions he would ask: Was there hard intelligence about the 317th MF Battalion? Could the unit be pinpointed? ("Don't hand me any center-of-mass crap, just tell me where the unit *is.*") What would be its likely avenues of escape when it learned the Riverine

Force had made it their target? For it was reasonable to assume that the battalion *would* find out that it was again a target.

The door to the S-2 Office sucks closed behind Claiborn. Two officers, one in khaki, the other in jungle fatigues, stand side by side in the harsh fluorescent light, both bent over a canted draftsman's desk covered with maps. It is cool here, absolutely quiet, wanting only muzak to complete the suggestion of an architect's office. The walls, painted a pale blue, are covered with line drawings of French cathedrals. From time to time the officers swing dividers and compasses over the maps or emplace red and blue pins in them. Occasionally they look at one another, pointing at a place on the map, and nod. They say very little.

The S-2 and his Navy counterpart Craig have a simple mission difficult of achievement: to establish beyond reasonable doubt the location of enemy units; at the very least to prepare reasoned defenses of their intuitions about where the enemy units are likely to move in the next few days. When they talk their conversation is brisk and official, thick with phrases like "the majority of the sightings would seem to indicate . . ." or "the LOC's have been getting heavy use" or "SLAR read-outs show that . . ." Each tiny fragment of "input"—information from every source at their disposal—is noted carefully in an intelligence journal and then plotted on the maps with the date of its receipt written beside it in ink. This results in the establishment of patterns as meaningless as Rorschach blots to

89

the lay observer, but to the intelligence men the clusters of colored pinheads tell a certain story of the activities of the Delta VC. Their guarded professional excitement at drawing careful conclusions from the arrangement of pins and plots and numbers on the maps may be compared to that of a historian whose researches have led him to inferences he finds inescapable. There is reduction to order; an intelligible pattern emerges.

Of course the fact that their intelligence estimates have taken the Riverine Force to one "dry hole" after another does not diminish their ardor or their enthusiasm. They enjoy a certain immunity from recrimination, for it is difficult to prove, after the event, that it was defective intelligence that resulted in the brigade's failure to make contact. Obviously, they argue, the VC were tipped off: *"They* found out we were coming." And so, in front of the nave of Beauvais Cathedral, they go on working and thinking and plotting.

Claiborn does not like them, and they do not like him. They resent his interruption.

"Dormeyer, I need everything you've got on the 317th Main Force Battalion."

"OK, everything I've got," the Major answers in his laconic and organized fashion. "A complete, verified OB. Strength 520 men. Twenty-eight separate sightings since 0600 6 March."

"What kind of sightings? Where?" Claiborn demands.

Dormeyer traces the suspected areas with his dividers, blocking off a rectangular piece of speckled light-green terrain three inches long by an inch wide on a one-to-fifty mapsheet. The ground, partly dense

90

jungle and partly mangrove, lies between two parallel rivers, the Rach Ba Nho and the Song Sao, both of them flowing west-east into a third stream, a broad river flowing south-north called the Giao Thong. In effect, the 317th appears to have occupied an inland peninsula: surrounded not by open water but by rivers ranging in width from 40 to 150 meters. Only the west end of the terrain pocket is open, but—as Claiborn recognizes at once—it is narrow enough for a blocking force to dominate. He therefore finds the intelligence hard to credit.

"Don't tell me the 317th'd hole up in a place like that."

"I'm telling you what the evidence tells me."

"How much of your evidence is radio intercepts?"

Dormeyer smiles in a sneering fashion at his examiner. "None of it."

It is obvious to him what Claiborn is getting at. Before TET it had been the clever tactic of the 317th and other Delta VC units to send communications squads into remote areas, have them come up on frequencies they knew the Americans were monitoring, and transmit messages all night, attempting to create the impression that their radio operators represented large VC units in established base areas. They did it well, too. For a time they had the Senior Advisor to IV Corps (an American major general) believing that several battalions of North Vietnamese regulars were at large south of the Mekong.

But tonight Dormeyer was more confident than ever. Trusted agent reports had come in, he said. The G-2 up at Division had even told him a LRRP patrol had brought in a Hoi Chanh, who had given him complete information on the battalion's strength and location and commanders. In spite of himself Claiborn found himself agreeing with the S-2.

"How late you staying up, Dormeyer? You expect more input tonight?"

"Probably. Where can I contact you—Plans shop?"

"Right. How about sending up your draft intelligence estimate for—what is it?—Kien Hoa Province. Be as detailed as you can be on the VC unit. Call me when you hear anything else."

But the S-2 has already turned back to his maps and is working away. Claiborn leaves. Again he makes his way through the ship, staring down naval ratings walking toward him along the passageways, back up through the wardroom, past the MARS station, and into the Plans Office, where he is not expected. The Plans drones, as Claiborn calls them, are watching a skin movie on the bulkhead—projected by an 8mm machine their gopher has just bought. A Negro woman is being laid by a white man in the back seat of a Hudson.

"Alright. Turn that goddamn thing off. Forrester, get out of here."

The projector is shut off, and the enlisted man leaves. Captain Knapp and Lieutenant Macarthy spin around on their office chairs and face the Major.

"Get up."

They stand up like schoolboys caught masturbating.

"What d'ya think Forrester thinks of you: two officers watching a stag movie with a Spec Four?"

Macarthy: "I don't know what he thinks, Sir."

"I'll tell you what's gonna happen. Someday you're gonna tell that kid to do something and he's gonna slap you on the back and tell you to 'cool it.' You watch that shit with him, he thinks he's your buddy. I don't have to tell you that."

He calms down a little. "Knapp: it's 2240. By 0600 I want a plan and a draft operations order on my desk. At 0730 we're going to brief the Colonel."

"Where we going?"

Claiborn picks up a mapboard and lays it on Knapp's desk. With a red grease pencil he colors in the S-2's plot of the 317th Battalion. "Right here."

"Airmobile assets?"

"We don't know yet. Configure two schemes of maneuver—more if you want. One for a two-battalion riverine insertion, another for a one-battalion riverine, one-battalion airmobile. The Colonel will try to get us an AHC, but you know how these things work."

"Yeah. I know how they work. Two battalions riverine."

"Configure for both."

"Alright."

"Alright, what?"

"Alright, Sir."

Within five minutes Major Charles Claiborn is in his stateroom with his bottle of Jim Beam, reading "The Ubiquity of the Administrative Role in Counterinsurgency." No use harrassing Knapp while he draws up a plan.

★ 11 ★

KNAPP, Macarthy, and Lieutenant Renfroe, USN, are seasoned Plans officers. All have been dreaming up schemes of maneuver—in the case of Renfroe naval support plans, riverine distance calculations, "beach" locations—for the better part of a year. They are competent practitioners of a challenging profession. Like Dormeyer's and Craig's, however, their absorption is almost wholly intellectual. They are playing a great chess game, trying to out-think an opponent who makes few mistakes. Their attitude toward success and failure is unambiguous: if their plans result in solid contacts with the VC they are exhilarated; if not—well, the intelligence was faulty, or the inherent limitations of the Force were responsible, or the commanders chose to modify the plans.

Although not by design, these officers are not often in the field. Occasionally they overfly the objective areas in helicopters or visit the riverine fire support bases, but as a rule their professional activities are confined to the Plans Office of the *Samson*. They work very hard for perhaps two days, preparing their plans and operations orders, and then, while the rest of the Force is out looking for the elusive VC, they relax in their comfortable offices, monitoring the radio nets of the attacking battalions, reading, writing letters, compiling unit histories, and preparing awards citations. Time passes slowly, and there is little relief from the tedium, so that after two or three days without having to prepare fresh plans they look forward to new orders from Major Claiborn and throw themselves into their work when the orders come.

The door to the Plans Office opens, and Major Dormeyer's enlisted aide walks in and hands Captain Knapp a draft intelligence estimate. The Captain lays it over the mapsheet and begins to read:

CONFIDENTIAL   DRAFT   CONFIDENTIAL
Department of the Army
Headquarters First Brigade, the Lionhead Division
APO San Francisco 95112
121800 March 1968

Intelligence Bulletin 19-68
Subject: Intelligence Estimate of Kien Hoa Province
REFERENCE: AMS 4117I, 4117II, 4117III, 4118II, 4118IV.

TERRAIN: Located on the coast of the South China Sea, its northern boundary 68 km. south of Saigon, the Province of Kien Hoa (hereinafter referred to as KH) comprises some 821 square mi. of rice-growing alluvium plain. Slopes are negligible, the average elevation of the province being less than two meters. Delimiting terrain features, the provincial boundaries, include the Song My Tho on the north, the Song Co Chien on the west, and the South China Sea in the east. Further terrain subdivision is engendered by major tributaries of the Mekong system. Population density: 725 psm.

Terrain largely silt-clay over bedrock; dry-season compactness of terrain gradually becoming less comprehensive. Rice-dikes average 1 m. above sea level at low tide. Foliage thick: some primary jungle nipa palm, sugar cane—these combining to restrict observation and fields of fire over large sections of the province. The province, exclusive of built-up areas, is thickly mined and booby-trapped.

WEATHER: In fifty-two of sixty years for which records have been kept, early April has been the major transitional period from the dry to rainy seasons. This year is exceptional in that the transition appears to have begun five weeks early. Windflow is now strongly from the southwest. Cloud cover in late afternoons will severely restrict aerial operations and visibility. Heavy P.M. rains can be expected on twelve of fifteen days. Temperature range: 80° to 102° F. Surface winds predominantly from SSW at 8–14 kts.

LIGHT DATA:

DATE	BMNT	SR	SS	EENT	MR	MS	MOON PHASE
12 Mar	0618	0705	1848	1938	0740	0014	1st QTR
13	0618	0705	1849	1938	0758	0059	
14	0617	0704	1849	1939	0910	0215	
15	0616	0703	1850	1939	1115	0357	HALF
16	0615	0702	1851	1939	1155	0430	
17	0615	9701	1852	1939	1235	0455	

GENERAL: KH is a major rear area-storage sector for VC MR II. Three large secret zones, CM 515315, 421278, 410205, are considered sites of considerable enemy caches of rice and ammunition and medical supplies. Identified units operating in targeted area include:

(1) 204th LF Bn
(2) G 311 Air Defense Company
(3) H 13 Medical Support Company
(4) G 380 District Company
(5) 317th MF Bn

The 317th MF Battalion: Strength, Composition, Locations:

A. The Battalion's total strength is estimated at 520. These are disposed in sub-units as follows:

> Headquarters Section: 35 (includes rcn platoon)
> Three Rifle Companies: ea 125
> Combat Support Company: 50
> Artillery Company: 55

B. Weapons: Estimated:

75mm	4
60mm Mort	10
82mm Mort	6
120mm Mort	?2
M-60MG (US)	?4
12.7 MG	unk
RPG	unk
.30 cal LMG	unk

97

C. Locations:

1. Sub-units are disposed as follows:

Hq Sec	?567351
1st Co	From 562359 to 570356
2nd Co	From 537357 to 538365
3rd Co	From 545354 to 554348

2. Company positions fronting on major rivers heavily fortified.

MISCELLANEOUS: Target area is wholly sympathetic to VC and may be expected to render active support to 317th Battalion. All adult males will therefore be detained, tagged, searched, and sent forward to designated FSB's TBA. All documents, weapons, and other captured materials will be tagged and sent forward with detainees. Detainee cards will be filled out in compliance w/ intell dir 305-C.

EEI: Following information will be reported immediately by all units:

(a) Detailed descriptions of enemy uniforms, insignia, equipment, and weapons.

(b) Antenna wire and Land lines by DTG Compass direction, incl wire-type and condition.

(c) Enemy attempts to enter friendly radio nets. Frequency and language.

(d) Enemy possession or utilization of protective masks.

ACKNOWLEDGE: G ROBERTSON
                    COL   USA

OFFICIAL: /s/ DORMEYER,
                S2

CONFIDENTIAL   DRAFT   CONFIDENTIAL
Gp-4.

The Pentagon has something of a panacea, it thinks. It is argued, of course—hammered out, debated, analyzed, finally approved and signed off. Telexed toward the gorgeous East on a secure net. Between a three-wood shot and a wedge, the Commander United States Forces Pacific hits on the phraseology of the implementing directive, swings, birdies, changes, scribbles. The message is retransmitted to the Seat of War. And the Admiral's wife reflects over her vichyssoisse at the Kahala Hilton that her husband seems terribly relaxed tonight. "Pleased as punch!" The pianist winks at them, puts an Eddie Duchin 'til ready in front of Anchors Aweigh and plays it neatly. On the parquet dance floor several couples smile over at the Admiral and his lady and clap.

The directive appears on the senior aide's desk at Headquarters, Military Assistance Command Vietnam, is carried down a hallway, and laid on another desk. Is read by the General. Good, he thinks. An emendation here, there, a briefing worked up for the Corps Commanders. Tennis, overflights, some good music and sleep. The sun rises on another day in the great headquarters, and the corps commanders arrive in freshly waxed H-model hueys, are saluted and greeted. Crisp words are exchanged, and the implementing orders are handed around. The senior Corps Commander—Commanding General, II Field Force—radios from his chopper that, thank you very much, his division commanders, the major generals, are to see him this afternoon.

Meantime he massages the order, working in the familiar "isolate, fix and destroy . . . criterion . . .

99

success . . . enemy killed by hostile fire." Now the major generals arrive at his headquarters, and he and his people brief them and hand around fresh copies— Welsh, Kroger, Martin, Lemming, the last of whom finds his own thoughts on the tactical situation are fully corroborated. He is reassured.

Down goes the order: to Colonel George Robertson, as we have seen; now oral, not written, transmuted into earthier, more impatient language: "You have one week to produce." And through this gentle interme- diary to Major Charles Claiborn (fine soldier, but still, at this level, in clean sheets every night). Through Claiborn, double-shunted, to the intelligence officers. And now, at last, to Captain Philip Knapp, Stanford '63, enjoying the twenty-sixth summer of his life in the Plans office of the U.S.S. Samson, APB-58, riding at anchor in the dark evening waters of the Mekong off the city of Sa Dec. PFC Compella, we are getting down to you: don't be impatient.

In fact, he is not impatient—apprehensive, but not impatient. Just now he is in the troop compartment of the Samson, watching "The Graduate" with the other members of his rifle company. It is hot and close in here, despite the air-conditioning, and he is sitting on linoleum, on a Dr. Pepper stain. Several decks above, Captain Knapp is fondling a new camera and reading his Intelligence Estimate. Major Claiborn is reading "The Ubiquity of the Administrative Role in Counter- insurgency." Shuffling George has finished chapter eleven of The Way We Live Now *and is dropping easily into deep sleep. Ashore, thirty miles down river,*

*General Lemming is following Jeb Stuart around
Meade's Army. Up at Field Force, Lieutenant-General
Rockacre is talking to Scotty Reston. COMUSMACV
is listening to the AFVN news at his villa in Saigon.
In Hawaii, Commander, United States Forces Pacific,
is shaving. And in Washington, the Joint Chiefs and
the clever Defense analysts are listening to a briefing
on multiple re-entry warheads. The President is talking
to Senator Ribicoff while treading water in his pool.*

*For the moment, then, it is Knapp's move. And in
his brain the opportunities for Paul Compella and
others of his rank and station to challenge other young
men are stirring fitfully into definition. In the meantime, PFC Compella, imagine you're Dustin Hoffman
screwing that classy thirty-eight-year-old bitch-kitty
and don't be impatient. They'll get to you.*

Knapp resents not seeing the end of the skin flick,
resents no longer having the leisure to fondle and
admire the new SRT-100 Minolta he has just bought,
resents not being able to write his fianceé. But time is
short; he decides to give the destruction of the 317th
MF Battalion his attention. Like Dormeyer's and
Craig's, his problem is simple: how can the two infantry
battalions of the Riverine Force (that is, Colonel
Robertson's brigade-minus) be introduced into the
target area in such a way that the enemy will not be
able to escape?

There is a serious ramification: how can the American
battalions get to the VC positions intact, without tipping off their intended area of operations, their objec-

tive? Should the riverine convoy be ambushed en route to the objective, the kind of success Colonel Robertson wants—and apparently needs—will be impossible. The same VC who will ambush the boats or create a hot LZ for a helicopter-borne force will radio back to the 317th that the enemy is coming. The 317th will clear the area, getting as far as possible away from navigable streams and prospective helicopter landing zones. The Force will come up with another dry hole, taking nasty ambush casualties into the bargain. (A direct hit on an Armored Troop Carrier, a "tango-boat," will cause fifteen or twenty casualties, disable the boat, dislocate the landing plan, perhaps kill the company or platoon commander.)

Knapp warms quickly to the intellectual demands of the task. From Dormeyer's intelligence estimate and from his own knowledge of northern Kien Hoa, he plots the probable VC positions on his planning map and reaches a preliminary decision: one of the two riverine infantry battalions *must* be airlifted into a blocking position between the Rach Ba Nho and the Song Sao,* somewhere in the open country three or four clicks west of their juncture with the Kinh Giao Thong. This must be the opening stroke of the operation. The enemy will then be blocked on all four "sides" of the terrain pocket they have foolishly, unaccountably, occupied. If there is efficient execution, good security, and rapid deployment of troops from the helicopter landing zones into their blocking positions, the ma-

* A map of the target area is on facing page.

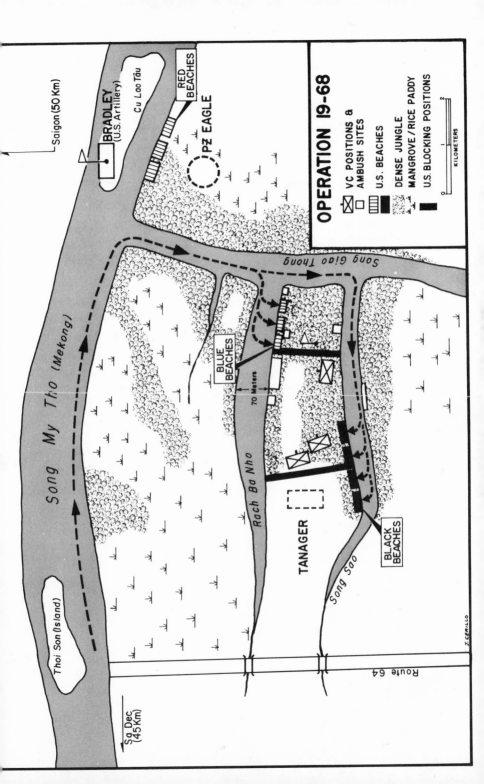

neuver will "seal" the VC in their base area, at the same time arresting the attention of those elements of the 317th disposed in bunkers along the rivers leading into the objective area, perhaps even drawing them away from these ambush sites.

He backtracks, thinking to himself: you underestimate the VC, Knapp. The plan will be simple, but its objects are not simple-minded men. Something more subtle is needed. He decides therefore to land a battalion off the boats five or six clicks away from the objective area. This will be the opening move. Put the battalion ashore and have them move inland just south of where the Giao Thong flows into the Song My Tho, moving to the open country which can serve as a helicopter pick-up zone. This battalion can then be airlifted from here and flown into the original blocking position. Get the VC thinking we are going to operate east of the Giao Thong, a reasonable feint, *then* establish the original block.

Meantime the second battalion can be brought into the objective area on the boats, landing on the north shore of the terrain pocket, beaching just short of the VC positions on the Rach Ba Nho. The gunboats—the "monitors"—can block off the waterways.

It is Major Claiborn's habit to ask Knapp, each time the latter prepares a plan, whether he will "stake his professional reputation" on it. Knapp reflects: yes, an unqualified yes (though he is leaving the Brigade for law school shortly, and he and Claiborn differ on what is meant by "professional reputation").

There is an unattractive complication, he remembers.

Claiborn had said there was no guarantee that the Brigade would be granted an AHC (a company of ten troop-carrying helicopters, each with a capacity of six fully equipped troopers). In this case the insertions would have to be wholly riverine. It would be disastrous, he decides; no surprise, heavy casualties, no way to block off the VC escape routes. He sees himself suddenly as a raging advocate arguing a case in front of Colonel Robertson: "Colonel, if you can't squeeze ten slicks out of General Lemming you'll lose half the Brigade." He must be prepared to argue in the morning that the operation should not be launched without a guarantee of helicopter support. In the meantime he can prepare a deliberately lame double riverine insertion plan.

"Jack," he turns to Macarthy, "get out warning orders to the 1st of the 71st and the 2nd of the 71st" (the designations of the two riverine battalions). "Have the message center get them out later tonight. The usual format. Tell them we'll launch probably the day after tomorrow—March 14th, sometime around 0400."

He and the Navy Plans officer then make some rough calculations. At the moment the ships of the Mobile Riverine Base are riding at anchor off Sa Dec, 45 kilometers from the target area. Plainly they must displace east down the Song My Tho tomorrow, the 13th, to their usual central anchorage just off Thoi Son island. That will put the force just 18 kilometers from the objective, still far enough away not to arouse VC suspicions unduly. Eighteen kilometers translate to about two and a half hours "sailing time" for the riverine boats, meaning the battalions can go aboard them around 0400 on the 14th, move downriver in the darkness, and arrive at their beaches shortly after sunrise. This will allow airstrikes and artillery preps on the beaches for fifteen or twenty minutes before D-hour.

The barge artillery—the old nemesis; the slower artillery barges must be in positions from which they can support the landings and subsequent operations at least forty-five minutes before the infantry lands. Knapp decides the floating batteries can be tied up on the North Bank of Cu Lao Tau island (from here their 9000-meter fans can "cover" the whole objective area). There is no way to avoid the risk of tipping the Brigade's hand: supposing a VC with a good radio is on the island. All he has to do is transmit the position of the artillery barges to the 317th (who must consider themselves the prime target in the central Delta), and the 317th can make good its escape before the blocking force can be inserted.

"The tyranny of the artillery," Knapp calls it. And yet the troops can't go into the objective without artillery cover. It is an article of faith, and a reasonable one. Knapp can only hope that the barges can take their positions unnoticed or that (small chance) the 317th will not consider themselves the likely target.

Time is slipping by. It is midnight, and the AFVN news has interrupted Jackie Gleason's "Music for Lovers Only" on the radio. The messages are familiar, only the numbers seeming to change. Knapp pauses to listen: ". . . elements of the 3rd Brigade, 4th Infantry Division, are reported to have killed twenty-seven Communists in heavy fighting in the central highlands. The

106

Communists left fifteen individual weapons on their positions. Friendly losses are described as light. In major-league baseball the Giants defeated the Cubs in their first meeting of the exhibition season, 6–1. Say, you know those big orange malaria pills? They can save your life. A pill a week is a small price to pay." There is a pause, and the signature music of another program of recorded music comes on: "The Dream of Olwen." All a strange pastiche, Knapp muses; and through it all, like garbled punctuation, can be heard the whiny voice of a soldier next door in the MARS (Military Affiliate Radio System) station. He is talking to his wife or girlfriend, and the hook-up is lousy, so he has to shout: "I *love* you, I *love* you. Can you hear me? Can you hear that?" A blast of static. "Yes, I'm fine, we're all fine here at home."

The Plans officer snaps back to the job, begins working on his operations order, typing it directly onto the stencil without making a draft, confident Colonel Robertson will buy off on it: he'll have to, Knapp reasons. Time is short, and only a madman would attack the 317th without helicopters.

In its complete form ninety minutes later the operations order—the written embodiment of Knapp's plan —looks like this:

CONFIDENTIAL   CONFIDENTIAL
          Copy #——— of 125 Copies
          Headquarters, Mobile Riverine Force
          TF 22, USN/Hqs 1st Bde, 12th Div.
          USS SAMSON, Sa Dec anchorage.
          13 March 1968

OPORD 19-68 (U)
Reference: Maps, Vietnam, 4117I, 4117II, 4118II
Time Zone: HOTEL
Task Organization
1st Battalion, 71st Inf (–)   *2nd Battalion, 71st Inf* (–)
1 AHC (TBA)
1st Plat, "C" Co, 25th Engr

Task Force Shotgun	*TF 22, USN*	*Brigade Control*
1st Bn, 19th Arty (–)		HHC, 1st Bde,
Co "C", 1st Bn,		Lionhead Div
71st Inf		Co "B", 2d Bn,
		71st Inf
		(MRB Defense)
		1 AHC (pass
		OPCON to
		1st/71st on
		order
		Troop,
		1st/9th Cav.

1. (C) SITUATION:
   a. Enemy Forces: Annex A—Intelligence Estimate 19-68 and Waterway intelligence bulletin dtd 1 Mar '68.
   b. Friendly Forces: N/A
   c. Attachments and detachments: See Task Organization, above, effective 132359 Mar.

2. (C) MISSION: MRF conducts riverine, airmobile search-and-clear operations in north central KIEN HOA Province to locate, fix, and destroy 317th VC MF battalion and other enemy elements in zone. Operation commences 140330 March.

3. (C) EXECUTION:

    a. Concept of Operation.

        (1) Scheme of maneuver: 2d Battalion, 71st Infantry (–), conducts riverine mvmt from MRB to Bchs RED 1, 2, 3, assaults same, moves on foot due east to PZ EAGLE. From EAGLE conducts airmobile mvmt to LZ TANAGER, thence establishing blocking positions oriented EAST, to prevent enemy exit from objective area. Alternatively, is prepared to land at Bchs BLACK 1, 2, 3, and engage enemy in zone. 1st Battalion, 71st Infantry (–), conducts riverine mvmt to Bchs BLUE 1, 2, 3, aslts same, and engages enemy in zone, sweeping west from Bchs (see mapsheet overlay atchd).

        (2) FIRES: ANNEX C, Fire Support Plan.

    b. 2d Battalion, 71st Infantry (–).

        (1) Conduct riverine mvmt from MRB to Bchs RED 1, 2, 3, commencing 140415 March.

        (2) Aslt Bchs 0715.

        (3) Move on foot to PZ EAGLE.

        (4) Conduct airmobile mvmt to LZ TANAGER.

        (5) Establish blocking positions oriented east between Rach Ba Nho and Song Sao.

        (6) On O, backload from Bchs TBA.

        (7) Coordinate with CTU 22. 1. 2 for riverine mvmt, fire support, and blocks.

        (8) Be prep to make initial landings at Bchs BLACK 1, 2, 3, if airmobile assets not avail.

    c. 1st Battalion, 71st Infantry (–).

        (1) Conduct riverine mvmt from MRB to Bchs BLUE 1, 2, 3, commencing 140345 March.

(2) Aslt Bchs 0715.

(3) Conduct search and clear opns oriented W and SW to engage enemy in zone.

(4) Coord organic fires w/ 2d battalion, 71st Inf.

(5) Backload on O, from Bchs TBA.

(6) Coord w/ CTU 22. 2. 1 for riverine mvmt, fire supt, blocks.

d. Co "B", 2d Bn, 71st Inf.

(1) Defend MRB.

(2) Coord w/ JTOC, USS SAMSON, for AOs and specific missions.

e. Task Force Shotgun.

(1) 1st Bn, 19th Arty (–).

(a) Conduct riverine mvmt from MRB to FSPB BRADLEY, commencing 140200 Mar.

(b) LRF at BRADLEY NLT 140700 Mar.

(c) Provide DS to 1st Bde (–).

(d) Coord w/ S-3, 1st Bde, for infantry elm.

(e) Rtrn to MRB on O.

(2) Co "C", 1st Bn, 71st Inf.

(a) Escort 1st Bn, 19th Arty to BRADLEY, secure and defend same on arrival.

(b) Coord w/ CTU 22.3. 1 for escort and lift.

f. AHC and 1st/9th Cav.

(1) Provide lift for 1st 71st Inf on O.

(2) Provide rcn for Bde as dir.

g. Coordinating instructions.

(1) SITREP/SPOTREP: S.O.P.

(2) Coordinate all fires within 400 mtrs of friendly boundaries.

(3) Evacuate all prisoners, detainees, wpns, and documents to FSPB BRADLEY

(4) Submit battalion plans to Plans Officer, 1st Bde, NLT 140000 Mar.

(5) MRB will relocate from SA DEC to THOI SON anchorage 131200 Mar.

(6) TF/BDE briefing 131700 U.S.S. *Samson.*

4. ADMINISTRATION AND LOGISTICS: ADMINO 1-68

5. (C): COMMAND AND SIGNAL.

  a. Command.

    (1) Bde CCB loc FSPB BRADLEY.

    (2) Bde C and C abn as required.

  b. Signal

    (1) Annex E, Signal.

Acknowledge: G. ROBERTSON
            Col
            A. JACOBS
            Captn USN

OFFICIAL: /s/ Knapp for Claiborn

  Group 4.

Downgraded in 3-year intervals.

Declassified after 12 years.

  DOD Dir 5200-10

★ 12 ★

AS we have seen, the Twelfth Division's area of operations was immense, half as big as New York State. Without dependable and efficient transport it is rotten country for Americans to fight in, and in the constant bickering over the limited helicopter resources (among all the divisions fighting in the southern portion of South Vietnam) there were days when the Twelfth Division had to make do without them. Of course it had "organic" helicopters which it could use in ash and trash missions, but nothing near the number required to fly battalions into combat.

Moreover, the AO was a natural field laboratory for new engines of war. Like phrases in search of ideas— to borrow a metaphor—the latest innovations in combat equipment were introduced to General Lemming's engineer officers and technicians, and they in turn tried to work up missions arguably suitable for them. The perversity of such a system needs little comment. For, as Robertson's planners were sketching out their conception of a battle without a morrow, a combined

ACSFOR-CDC team was bedding down for the night in air-conditioned luxury at Division after their first day in-country. They had come to oversee the combat employment of three new machines of war transport.

The machines appeared to be militarized versions of the Channel hydrofoils—squat stubby amphibians with huge fans mounted astern, their olive-drab skins already set off with the inevitable shark's teeth and their superstructures flying American and confederate flags. Each machine was supposed to be able to carry a small number of infantry plus its crew, and each disposed M-60 machine guns and an automatic grenade launcher. Supposedly the machines could travel at sixty or seventy miles an hour over open water and somewhat less over rice paddy, including the lower rice-dikes. The Washington people and Lemming's G-3 officers set about figuring what to do with them.

A study of the machines' characteristics led to several conclusions. They were too unproved to go out alone; too small to carry recon parties larger than those the hueys customarily "inserted" into the AO; too ponderous of maneuver to be trusted in any but the broadest streams of the river system or the most open country (they changed direction rather like hand-held floor-waxers); too noisy to perform useful reconnaissance missions.

So a mission was developed which could take advantage of all these non-performance factors. The CDC team chief had been reading Bruce Catton on the long flight out, and a phrase had stuck in his mind: Lee could take risks at Chancellorsville precisely because his position was desperate; there was no rational tactic to throw against Joe Hooker. As the CDC man understood it, Lee saw himself as a man whose commitment and intuitions would be vindicated in the event, despite the odds, the figures, the careful calculations. It struck him that the problem with his machines was similar. The thing was an unproved gadget to which the Army had committed itself, intuiting that it would do useful work. Almost anything, therefore, should be claimed for it to assure it got proper field tests. The machine would prove their instincts were sound.

After an hour's discussion of the Chancellorsville campaign with the G-3, the CDC team chief was delighted to find the former prepared to recommend a combat mission for one of the machines to General Lemming.

This was fortuitous. That morning the General had received a letter from his old Benning friend Phil Regan, Commanding General, CDC. Regan's note had concluded:

> George, we're not sure about this thing, but we have a hunch it'll be useful. We want it to get a chance. Much time and money have gone into the project and now's a bad time to turn back. See that it gets a decent work-out and let me know what we can do to help your people if bugs develop.

Be it noted, by the way, that Phil Regan, a lieutenant general, was sitting on a small and recently convened board of senior generals to consider officers for appointment to three-star rank, and that George Lemming was not unaware of this fact. He expressed delight with the

G-3's recommendation for a mission for one of the machines.

It would pick up a squad of Division recon troopers on the night of 12-13 March, carry the squad down one of the long reaches of the Ham Luong River and put it ashore, proceed from there along a narrower tributary to conduct reconnaissance, attempt to "flush VC," and stop and search any waterborne traffic foolish enough to be out after the twilight curfew. Five hours later it would return to the original off-load point for the recon people, pick them up, and return to base.

It set out shortly after Colonel Robertson had returned from Division to the Sa Dec anchorage. Within three hours, at the same time Claiborn was admonishing the Plans officers for watching dirty movies in the presence of enlisted people, it lay dead in the water with an apparent "transmission malfunction." The lieutenant in command at once broke radio silence and called the G-3 project officer in the Division Tactical Operations Center, who had stayed up with the G-3 and the G-2 to monitor the mission. By midnight an angry George Robertson had been awakened and had decided to commit a rifle company to protect the stricken craft. This unit, one of Lieutenant Colonel Plowman's 1st Battalion, 71st Infantry, rode a small riverine convoy to the machine and occupied the riverbanks on either side of it.

By first light, 13 March, the danger of the machine's being ambushed now somewhat dissipated, the company commander had reported that he had secured it, and that in the process he had taken one killed and five wounded from a booby-trap, and two killed by the fires of the machine, whose commander had ordered it to shoot at suspicious noises on the bank.

There it would sit for another day, tied to a tree. The combined efforts of the CDC technicians and their protégés from Division could not get it working. Meantime the infantry company took two more wounded from another booby-trap. Not until the second day could a CH-54 flying crane helicopter be coaxed out of II Field Force to lift the crippled machine out of the river and fly it back to a repair complex outside Saigon.

Those under the crane's line of flight on the morning of 15 March would see a bizarre sight: at 1800 feet the crane batting its way along, a lugubrious flying beast dangling the broken machine below it in lazy arcs. A million dollars' worth of technology (or was it only $650,000?) advertising its own absurdity. One imagined a VC leaning back against a tree, cleaning his ancient surplus carbine, looking up and wondering if the machine were some new kind of bomb.

General Lemming's comment to G-3: "Why'd you let the son of a bitch into the AO if it wasn't going to work?" And a note to Phil Regan: "The machines appear to have a minor transmission bug which we're getting sorted out just now at Long Binh. We have high hopes for them, especially when the monsoon season gets far enough advanced to ground the choppers in the afternoon. . . . Do give my love to Paula."

✶ 13 ✶

USS Samson, APB-58
0630, 13 March 1968

AT 0600 precisely Captain Knapp, arms full of planning maps and operations orders, knocks on Major Claiborn's stateroom door, and without waiting for an answer opens it and goes in. Do not imagine Claiborn is curled up, defused, like a small boy on his bunk. No. Knapp looks down at the floor, sees before him, poised on its toes and fingertips in the front-leaning-rest position, the muscular hairy body of his boss. The Major is just finishing his push-ups. At the sound of the door opening he springs to his feet. Knapp sees that he has already shaved and that there are no sleepers in his eyes. He wears tan gymshorts and a grey T-shirt with "A A A" stamped on the chest, and he is not in the least embarrassed by the intruder.

"Up early, ay, Sir?"

Claiborn does not answer, slams open a desk drawer, takes out a hand and forearm squeezer, and begins scrunching it with his left hand. With the other hand he disengages a collapsible easel from behind the bunk. "Put your planning map on that and brief me," he orders. He sits down on the bunk.

Knapp talks uninterruptedly for twenty minutes, taking Claiborn through the whole planning sequence, pointing out the VC positions, the liabilities of terrain and waterways in Kien Hoa, reciting the tide and sunrise tables, finally tracing on the acetate the fire support plan and the proposed scheme of maneuver. The briefing is crisp, polished, assured. He looks at Claiborn for reactions.

"You know Knapp, you oughtta go Regular. Y'ever think about it? That's a good goddamn plan."

Knapp wonders aloud if Claiborn has ever heard of Robert M. Hutchins. "You know what he once said? Whenever he got the urge to exercise he lay down until it passed. You know what I mean?"

"I catch your drift, smart-ass." Claiborn is suddenly in a good mood, looser. The plan strikes him as a perfect mix of simplicity and complexity: simple for the Brigade to execute, difficult for the VC to react to. "But think about going RA. You know what they say: travel, adventure, retirement . . ."

"Yes, Sir, good retirement. Ride shotgun on a garbage truck."

"OK, Knapp, that'll do."

"Each to his own."

Claiborn springs off the bunk, slaps his hands together. "So much for that. I agree about the airmobile assets. We can sell the Colonel on it. The riverine

118

gambit's counterproductive in this situation. You want me to brief the Colonel and the Commodore?"

"You got the clout, you brief them. I'll leave the operations order and the planning map here. I've signed the OP order and the annexes for you, and the Navy's approved everything. I'm gonna sleep for an hour."

"Meet me in the Colonel's stateroom at 0730, right?"

"Good, Sir."

The Major turns the easel toward him, pulls it closer. Arms folded across his chest he stares at it for fifteen minutes.

Captain Alden Jacobs IV, USN, by courtesy and traditional usage addressed as "Commodore" (being in command of several capital ships) and Colonel George Robertson, USA, the joint commanders of the Mobile Riverine Force, share a suite of staterooms well forward in officer country on the *Samson*. Davitt and Company, Naval Engineers and Shipbuilders, who refitted the *Samson* for its second war, had been told the vessel was to be a command ship housing both naval and military persons, and they subcontracted the decorating chores to John Wanamaker in Philadelphia. The latter undertook to see that the staterooms of these officers were comfortably and tastefully appointed.

The Commodore and the Colonel presently occupy sleeping-quarters on either side of a combination study and dining room. The appointments of Captain Jacobs' sleeping-quarters had been subtly rendered in blue and gold—a clever stroke prompted by the attendance of the Wanamaker man at an Army-Navy football game. Brass miniature anchors and Naval Academy beer mugs rest on a narrow shelf which runs around the wall of the stateroom just below the "overhead." The walls (the bulkheads) are covered with ersatz knottypine; the floor with thick pile carpeting in cobalt blue. In a small alcove next to the Commodore's dresser stands a government-issue desk, on the left back corner of which is a lamp-stand of enameled terra-cotta wrought into a figure of a drunken sailor leaning against a lamp-post. His outstretched right hand holds a light socket.

A set of books, handsomely bound in Navy blue, occupies the shelf above the desk, none of them, judging from their perfect order, ever having been read by the present occupant of these quarters: the soothing ruminations of Captain Mahan; Puleston's *Life* of that great strategist; Corbett's *Some Principles of Maritime Strategy;* a thick *History of Amphibious Operations of the Russo-Japanese War;* Southey's *Life of Nelson;* Smollett's *Roderick Random;* a *Hornblower Anthology;* and Michaelson's *Byrd: Polar Penetrator.*

The desk itself is littered with private correspondence, tide tables, RAND studies of the Mekong Delta and the VC, a Groton Alumni Bulletin. To the right, under a porthole, is a framed National Geographic Society map of Southeast Asia, on which Vietnam appears as a narrow orange appendix clinging to a less brilliantly colored mainland.

Out of these quarters, at 0731, steps the Commodore: a Michenerian naval officer, thin and hard, crows-footed under a handsome facial tan. He has a thick crop of Kennedy hair and is immaculate in fresh service khaki. Drawling, he greets his visitor thus: "Claiborn, how are you this morning? Nice t'see you. Have a seat until the Colonel joins us and ask the other plans and operations people in."

The sounds of the Colonel's ablutions can be heard from the other stateroom. Shuffling George is preparing for the new day. His room is standard don't-give-a-shit deshabille: dirty fatigues piled in a corner, pistol belt and .45 hanging from a bulkhead, ashtrays filled with burnt-down cigar butts, paperbacks everywhere. Except for their titles, the ambience is midwest locker room: brass cannon and West Point beer mugs on the shelves, a World War I doughboy supporting a light-socket on the end of a bayonet, sienna-brown pile carpeting. This stateroom, too, has its TO & E books, bound in maroon: biographies of military heroes: Heinz Guderian, Chinese Gordon, Douglas Macarthur; a Clausewitz; deGaulle's *Memoirs*. They too are unread. On the floor, by the head of the bunk, are *The Way We Live Now* and *Couples*.

Now Shuffling George enters the sitting-room, blinking against the dazzling morning sun in the porthole. He must be accounted combat ineffective until after two cups of coffee and ten Camels, but he manages, "Hi, Charles, you ready?" and Claiborn, always ready, steps smartly to his portable easel, props up Knapp's planning map of Kien Hoa, and begins the briefing.

"Commodore, Colonel, Captain Knapp has developed what I think is an excellent plan. I will go through the projected sequence of proposed operations on the assumption that you both have seen copies of last night's intelligence bulletin." Robertson nods; the Commodore waves his hand airily in assent.

"We are presently anchored at Sa Dec, 45 kilometers from the proposed target. The ships would displace late this morning to the Thoi Son anchorage. At 0300 tomorrow morning the artillery barges will leave (subtly the tense modulates from would to will) the MRB and move to the north coast of Cu Lao Tau island, from which they can support our operations in the objective area.

"At 0415 the 2nd of the 71st will debark the MRB, load the CTU 22. 1. 2 tango boats, and move to Beaches RED 1, 2, 3 (he points them out on the map). After assaulting the beaches the battalion will move inland to pick-up zone EAGLE, there to begin an airmobile lift into landing zone TANAGER. From here the battalion will fan out and assume blocking positions oriented east, thereby precluding VC egress from the TAOR . . ."

He looks directly at Colonel Robertson, waiting for his reaction to the helicopters. The Colonel's face seems a caricature of Broderick Crawford's: pleased with the initiative of a well-loved subordinate, whimsically frowning at the latter's faith in him.

"As yet I have no hard promise of airmobile assets," Robertson declares quietly.

"You can get the helicopter company, can't you, Sir?"

Three or four seconds of silence. The smoky bonhomie of the conference suddenly yields in a flash to an unmistakable voice, magisterial, hard, positive.

"No, he can't get them, Major."

George Simpson Lemming regards the group from the passageway, his aide standing behind him with a clipboard. No one had noticed the distant shudder of a helicopter settling down on the flight deck of the ship. The officers rise quickly, and he comes in.

Lemming orders them to "siddown." Then, "Commodore" (studiously he ignores Robertson) "you'll get a TWX on this within the hour. You have a distinguished visitor coming aboard this afternoon. Code name: Blue Streak. The Secretary of the Navy. I think you knew he was in-country? COMNAVFORV called me at 0700 and I flew out as soon as he hung up."

"He asked me what you had in the works. I told him I was uncertain, but that I expected you and Robertson were mounting an operation in the next day or two . . ."

The officers catch the meaning of his words before he says anything more, but he continues, inevitably. "The last thing in the world your boss wants is an airmobile operation by the *riverine* force while Mr. Ignatius is here. It's as simple as that."

As simple as that. The Navy pours a mint into the Mobile Riverine Force, tells the Secretary of Defense the Force is perfectly tailored to work with the Army in the Delta, is giving the embarked troops perfect, unstoppable mobility. How could the Secretary of the Navy fly to Vietnam to be shown that the MRF—as if publicly to confess its wretched tactical failures—was depending on an Army helicopter company to get its embarked troops into objective areas?

Robertson: "Goddamit, General, the operation we've

planned is suicidal without airlift. We've got what appears to be a hard fix on the 317th. We can probably clean their clocks for good. But we've *got* to have air-mobile support. Were you standing there long enough to hear the Major's briefing?"

"Most of it. It's a good plan. But you'll have to put both battalions on the boats. I've already given the AHC to 3rd Brigade."

Robertson is not a shouting man. The General has come to a certain decision, and it will stand. Lemming has no intention of poisoning an amicable working relationship with COMNAVFORV (a three-star admiral) for the sake of a single brigade operation. But Robertson, not yet thinking clearly in the early morning, ignores his instincts and plunges:

"You want a casualty estimate right now? I'd guess 50 to 75 killed (US), 150 to 300 wounded. The boats'll get the shit shot out of them and the VC'll unass their main positions before the boats get the troops anywhere near them. The Kien Hoa waterways are solid ambush sites without exception. The operation is dangerous enough with one battalion *airlifted* in. Without choppers the mission's a complete bust."

Lemming stands with his hands on his hips and fixes Robertson with his standard pre-explosion stare. "The decision's final, Colonel. Commodore, it shouldn't upset you especially."

Jacobs shrugs, looking down at the floor. "I'm obliged to follow the Army Plans recommendations, General. We have no particular expertise in military tactics. The prospects for the boats and sailors are as bad as they are for the troops. Does COMNAVFORV have any idea what they'll be getting into?"

Lemming, disappointed in not finding an ally, answers resignedly: "He has an idea. You and George here will have to massage the plan you've got and do the best under the circumstances. I don't have to remind you that what's at issue here transcends the significance of a single operation." He looks pleasantly at Major Claiborn. "Chick, you can work up something decent with the boats, can't you? Do they have to go up the Giao Thong? Could you get access to the AO from the south?"

"It's not practical, General. We considered that option last night."

"Well, do what you can. I don't suppose it makes any sense to postpone the exercise. The VC aren't going to stay in there very long." He stares abstractedly out the porthole. The surface of the river is shimmering with the sun and the rising heat, and the sounds of working-parties drift up from the pontoons below. The stateroom is absolutely quiet, the officers staring down at the table. What can they say to Lemming? It is not so much that they feel professionally debarred from criticizing his hideously poor decision as that they know he has made his mind up. Why should a drunk scream in a padded cell?

Lemming leaves and the ship soon begins to shudder as his chopper starts turning over.

Shuffling George remembers having seen the Secretary of the Navy in a Pentagon lunch-room, and recalls his friendliness and charm. He was said to be a reasonable and compassionate man, which, Robertson now reflects, probably means that the Navy brass finds him easy to handle. But . . . reasonable. He'd probably be the last man in the world to endorse the kind of operation his troops are about to undertake; and yet, for his "benefit," it will be launched. Chin in hand, Robertson looks over at Claiborn and his young Captain Knapp. The latter's face tells a story of disbelief, disappointment, rage.

"Charles," he says, "you and Knapp and Renfroe scheme the plan for two battalions riverine. I guess you'd better make the 1st of the 71st the lead battalion. They've been in there before."

"They're understrength, Colonel."

"I know that. So's the other battalion."

The Commodore puts down his coffee mug. "Well, let's have at it. I'm sorry, George." And he is.

On the AMMI pontoon tied up below Paul Compella is throwing a frisbee to his squad leader.

THREE

A Real Sharp Individual

There's two million men have fought out there, and their performance has been magnificent. Mention a battle they've ever lost in Vietnam.

MAXWELL TAYLOR TO INTERVIEWER
Issues and Answers, 4 July 1971

✶ 14 ✶

PAUL Compella was born in Torrington, Connecticut, on February 1, 1948, and was named for his grandfather who had come to this country from Livorno in 1905. He was baptized at St. Peter's Church, and had what may be called a conventional Catholic boyhood in an industrial New England city.

While he was growing up his father worked steadily at Scovill's and his mother was active in the Church. Their son attended a local parochial school through the eighth grade, neither distinguishing nor disgracing himself. In his post-adolescence he would remember little of those years: self-absorbed service as an altar boy at St. Peter's; the all-night burn of chlorine in his eyes after work-outs at the "Y" pool; the unshakable certainty that the Yankees would pull it out in the bottom of the ninth at the Stadium; the lash of a rosary around his neck for laughing in class . . .

He went to Torrington High School. At fifteen, only a sophomore, he made the state Class "A" second-team all-star basketball team, its youngest and smallest member. He was elected vice-president of his class. Next year he took his SAT's, scoring 505 in the verbal portion, 445 in mathematical aptitude. It was about that time, '64, that the student athletes at the High School were turning away from Villanova and Boston College and Holy Cross and starting to apply to Yale and Dartmouth. "You don't want to go to the Cross, huh? Well, of course Gus Broberg went to Dartmouth, and you're far enough into the woods there it doesn't matter if your fly's unbuttoned."

Compella dated a pretty cheerleader, the daughter of a surgeon. They were in love, but no one knew about it until he broke the jaw of a friend who asked him whether the girl "put out." It is the only violent thing anyone now living in Torrington can remember him doing.

His last year at the High School was one of fulfillment and terrible disappointment. He was captain of the basketball team which finished runner-up to New Haven Hillhouse in the state finals, was voted most popular boy in his class, made Mayor for a Day by the Exchange Club, and within the space of a week was rejected by Dartmouth, Penn, Michigan, and Holy Cross. It was a humiliation he had no idea how to accept. Meantime students he knew only vaguely ran about the halls waving their acceptances: pale unpopular types who had never even sat in the bleachers to watch the team play. After graduating, Compella worked that summer on the County roads for Oneglia and Gervasini, quitting his job late in September to attend the Torrington branch of the University of Connecticut.

By now, however, the thrust, the drive, the quiet pride of his high-school years had deserted him. The girl had gone to Manhattanville College and did not write him. His parents got on his nerves; it was no good trying to study at night in the living room with the TV going, and it was unpleasant to argue with his father about when he could use the car.

A solution appeared in the form of a letter from his draft board in November 1966, and he began recruit training at Fort Polk, Louisiana.

Paul was a good recruit—too young, a bit too dull to be cynical, too proud to show the homesickness that had him crying silently at night in the squad-bay. His athletic gifts saw him through the experience successfully. Wiry and agile, he set a speed record on the obstacle course, qualified expert with the M-14, and was formally recognized eight weeks later as honor graduate of his training company. After two weeks' leave in Torrington, most of which he spent at home in bed, he reported to Fort Benning for paratroop training and from there he joined an airborne battalion in the 82nd Division.

At Bragg he had the usual experiences of a young soldier in a stateside infantry unit. From time to time he got drunk; he lost his virginity to a whore in Kinston, North Carolina, made fifteen parachute jumps with his company—some from C-141 jets—and received the Division's RECONDO badge and the inevitable orders to Vietnam on the same day. He had expected the orders and regretted only that he was not going over with his own company.

About "Vietnam" (the connotations of the word were

suddenly widening) he had not thought seriously. It was something to be got through, and he supposed they wouldn't have sent him unless it was necessary that he go there. Most of his friends in the 82nd were either resigned to it, or curious to test themselves in it, or downright eager to get to the war. It was the year, of course, of the First Air Cav Division, when even *Time* was writing admiring articles about a new young military professionalism, about lean and fit marine battalions and daring new battle tactics and sophisticated weapons. Captain Donlin had come home to the Congressional Medal of Honor and there was a colored picture of him in the company office: sober, becomingly abashed, blue-eyed. The *Green Berets* was out in paperback; and Captain Pete Dawkins, according to *Life,* "kept on winning."

The staff NCO's he knew around the company had already been once and had returned, tough quiet paratroopers who read copies of the *Daily News* in the doors of C-130's before jumping out. They talked about their war experiences as though they were part of a longish football game interrupted by a week or so at places like Kuala Lumpur and Hong Kong and Tokyo.

They always tried to get beer to you in the boondocks. "We went eight weeks without *seein'* a VC once." Walk around, keep your eyes open, set up at night (artillery registered all around the company position), sack out, walk around . . . "When the mortars come in on you at night, man, get down in your hole or lie flat on your stomach because y'ain't so vulnerable in the ass and, you know, your back muscles are strong and the shrapnel don't get in deep there."

And, "Bull fuckin' shit, Sergeant Creese. What the fuck you tellin' those people? Shit. Shrapnel goes through a Green Bay Packer just like it goes through you." Everyone laughed. Bull fuckin' shit. "Most guys who got it I knew got it in the last two months . . . they get too loose then. You know, they think they got it made. But you ain't got it made until you get on that freedom bird at Bien Hoa. Don't forget that. They took ten rounds one night at Bien Hoa, and this MI lieutenant got some steel in his leg. You know what he did? He wrapped his undershirt around it and changed his khakis and got on the plane in the morning. And he waited until that plane was 20,000 feet up and halfway to Travis before he told the stewardess he got shot. He wasn't gonna stay in no hospital in Bien Hoa. No way."

Compella went back to Torrington for his thirty-day pre-combat leave. For the first time the town struck him as grimy and tight. Carol, the Manhattanville girl, had taken up political science in college. She regarded him as a fit object for "creative radicalization."

"How can you shoot some woman or farmer?"

To which Compella gave the stock answer. "Depends on the wind that day. Like, if it's ten miles an hour, lead 'em three clicks windage at 200 yards." But he was ashamed as soon as he'd said it.

The girl had neither the knowledge nor the conviction to work on him very hard. She would marshal her facts on the way to the Torrington Drive-in and in between flicks would tell him how corrupt the French had been and how Ho Chi Minh really had tried to stop the massacre of the 50,000 Vietnamese who had collaborated with them; how it was a civil war fought by nationalists who had only had old rifles and no nay-plam (she called it) of their own. And how it made her sick that Johnson with his stupid gall bladder scar and his basset hounds was sending boys a third as old as he was to die there.

On the night before Paul flew to San Francisco his mother and father got Carol over for dinner with the rest of the family. The evening was not successful: Frances Compella in the kitchen crying off and on, his father's voice with the catch in it every time he tried to say something important, their retreat upstairs at eleven, the wrestling on the couch in front of the late show. Later the girl ran up the sidewalk to her house without kissing him good-bye; and much later, waking him out of a fitful sleep at 3 A.M., she called him and told him to take care of himself.

In the morning they drove out to Bradley Field, near Hartford, Paul looking spruce and clean in his para-trooper gear: boots, cords, fouragerre, wings. He checked in his bags, hugged his mother a long time, accepted two twenties from his father who told him, trying to be tough and affectionate at once, to "watch your ass." The remainder of his journey to Vietnam later blurred in his memory: 190 men in a purple Braniff stretch-jet; a layover on Guam watching B-52's take off on their bombing missions; conventionally kind, tart-assed stewardesses who treated the young soldiers as though they were changing bedpans in a terminal cancer ward; the sudden closeness and black of the un-loading zone at Bien Hoa.

He was in Vietnam.

134

★ 15 ★

U.S.S. Samson, APB-58
Sa Dec Anchorage, Mekong River
0900, 13 March 1968

"HOW often do we go out? How often does the company go on operations?" PFC Compella is talking to his friend Provenzano, both of them sitting in the back row of a group of new men drawn up in a semicircle around their First Sergeant, who is explaining how to clean M-16's and M-79's in the Delta. To his students the lecture has the interest of the flip-side of a hit record.

"Once, maybe twice a week. Two or three days each."

The First Sergeant has overheard them. "What's your name, clown?"

"Provenzano, First Sergeant."

"Who's your buddy there?"

"PFC Compella, First Sergeant."

"You think because my name ends in a vowel like yours you're gonna get favors out of me your head's up your ass. You got that?"

Compella and Provenzano nod at him.

"Your weapon don't fire you're a dead man, you got that?"

Compella nods.

"Do you?"

"Yes, First Sergeant."

"You come here on levy from the airborne?"

"Yes, First Sergeant."

"Shit. That ain't gonna do you no good here. A unit parachute into Kien Hoa or Ba Xuyen, they'd stick in up to their neck." The rest of the new-in-countrys look around at Compella and laugh.

Sergeant Bromleo is having a rough time getting through to his people, most of them fascinated by their new surroundings. The *Samson* is barely 150 meters from the north shore of the Mekong, and it has swung around on its anchor so that the Sergeant's back is to the shoreline. The soldiers look past him, at the two tango boats idling upriver, at the Monitor doing laps along the shore, protecting the MRB anchorage. The shore is dazzlingly bright, solid inpenetrable jungle shining bright green to chrome yellow. Somewhere in there, not far, one of the other companies of the battalion is on the MRB security perimeter, though Compella can't imagine how a couple of gooks with B-40's couldn't get through, sidle patiently through the undergrowth and deadfall, and put a round through the *Samson* or one of the LST's.

He wonders about swimmers, too. Couldn't some VC in Scuba gear, or something, come up under the hull and stick one of those limpet mines to the ship? It is an unsettling thought, but it has never happened.

The First Sergeant's demonstrators have reassembled the two weapons and the Sergeant is discussing the M-16. "This little bastard may look frail. Did anybody here ever see a man wounded by one?" A few hands are raised, some lazily, some proudly. "What the round'll do, it'll like oscillate in the air, it's so light, and when it gets in you it don't make a clean wound, but tears your insides up. There's a man got med-evacked last week from the 2nd of the 71st. Charlie got him with an M-16 some little fart left behind and the round went into his thigh and came out his back, above the spine . . ."

Compella and the others hear nothing of the next thirty seconds of the lecture; instead they try to figure out the course of the M-16 round inside the soldier from the 2nd of the 71st. They all conclude that the soldier will never be able to get laid again.

"So keep the son-of-a-bitch clean, and for Christsake don't lose it. Also, you'll be told when to fire it on full and when to fire it on semi. Is there any questions?"

Sergeant Bromleo introduces one of the battalion medics. "I am Specialist Five Bohuncker and today I am going to brief you on foot diseases in the Delta. Pay attention and you can avoid this."

From the first row of listeners a PFC who has been hunkered down through the Bromleo pitch leaps to his feet and pulls up his left pant leg to the knee. He kicks the diseased leg out and back like a chorus girl, the ankle and calf covered with ten or fifteen oval-shaped sores on which scabs have not formed. Around the edges the sores are the color of pus. The rest of the exposed part of the leg appears to have been painted

137

with a calomine-like lotion. The display has the desired effect; it arrests the revolted attention of the soldiers.

"When're you due to rotate, Simmons?"

"Next Tuesday."

"OK, that's a week from now. Add maybe six weeks on to that. He'll be home in the States six weeks and he can't do shit because of his leg. Tell these people how your leg got like that."

"Goin' out on one fuckin' operation after another one."

"Besides that, smart-ass." Nobody loves a smart-ass.

"Didn't wash off in the field. Didn't cut holes in my jungle-fatigue pants. Didn't go on sick call. Didn't change my socks."

"Y'hear that? He didn't wash hisself or change his socks or go on sick call. You agents do what he did and your legs'll be like his." He pauses and looks at Simmons, who has pulled down his pant-leg and is back sitting with the group. "I might say that Simmons is going home with more than a leg like that. He got the Silver Star in My Tho during TET, but his leg was OK then, right Frank?"

"Right."

The medical spiel lasts another half hour and concludes with the inevitable VD pitch. "You come to me or Doc Adams with the clap don't tell me you got it off no toilet seat. Where you're goin' there ain't gonna be no toilet seats, one, and, two, slope pussy ain't worth the effort. There's one way to avoid the clap, and that's to lay off innimit contact with indigenous females."

A hand goes up. "Is that true the third time you get clap they clean you out with a rotary blade?"

138

"I'll tell you what. You believe that's what we do and there won't be any third time, alright?"

The new man grins sheepishly.

"R and R, the rate varies. Australian girls are clean, most of 'em. Hong Kong and Manila you're asking for it. One other thing. Men ask me what is their pussy cut-off date. I would allow a good four-five weeks anyway. You don't wanna find you got no drip at the Podunk airport."

In a way Compella finds this portion of the briefing reassuring. Simmons goes home next Tuesday; the medic talks about R and R (for most of the new soldiers a good five or six months away) as though they will all be around to enjoy it; PCOD's for men going home. Well, the odds are good. Torrington is cruddy at this time of year, the late winter snows coming as afterthoughts, caking grimily around the hydrants and curbs. What you needed in Torrington was a car. Let's see, save $225 a month for a year, that would be almost $2700, less maybe $400 for R and R. That would buy a '65 Electra outright. Fat city. He imagines himself driving the Electra back down to Bragg after his thirty-day leave, back to the last three months of Army service, stopping off maybe at Philly and D.C. Two decks of ribbons and a CIB. And then maybe another shot at those colleges.

He looks down at his jungle fatigues. How long will it take these things to fade?

". . . and you too, Compella. I can see you and me's gonna go round-and-round you don't listen up. What the hell am I talking to you people for, my health? Now, I'm gonna introduce Lieutenant Haney, Platoon leader, 1st Platoon, Company "A". You don't go to sleep on no officer. Lieutenant Haney's briefing is on infantry tactics. Listen up."

Lieutenant Ralph R. Haney, IV: tall, about six feet, and lean, sunburned like a Moor; University of Michigan '66, co-captain of football, majored in history. He is relaxed, poised, confident, formerly a General's aide and like Compella an ex-82nd Division man. The troops study him carefully.

"First Sergeant Bromleo, gentlemen, welcome to the Company. I want you to look on either side of yourselves. Learn the face of the man on either side of you. Because in six months, if history means anything, one of the two people you're sitting next to is going to be a dead man or badly wounded."

The Lieutenant pauses, letting the awful words sink in. He is only repeating what he once heard another officer tell a class of second lieutenants at Fort Benning. That was a year ago, and in the hallway later the second lieutenants scorned the warning as panache, a cheap shot. Nor did it enter their minds that any of them would die in Vietnam. War remained somewhat remote in Georgia.

Haney has seen the warning borne out during TET, and his words to the troops, if they represent a questionable psychology, are honest. Compella, on the other hand, looks immediately at First Sergeant Bromleo. So do the rest of the troops. They study him, looking for a changed expression—a frown, a suppressed grin, a shrug, the blinking of an eye—which will reassure them that the Lieutenant's a bullshit artist, that what he has just said is only an attention-getting step which might have been a dirty joke. But Bromleo's expression does not change; he does not move, only continues to look at the Lieutenant. Haney's observation must be true, they decide: 50 percent killed or wounded in the next six months.

"And a lot of the people who got it got it because they didn't pay attention to what they were taught. Now, we're in the field maybe three days out of six. We come out of the field and get cleaned up and eat well. And the ship is air-conditioned. But in my platoon, and I think I can speak for the whole company as well, those three days out of the field are not free time. There will be classes like these every day you're not on working parties or getting ready for operations. Pay attention to what's said. You can learn from the men who are going to talk to you. The NCO's and officers who wear the Lionhead (he points at Bromleo, whose left breast pocket features a sewn depiction of a lion leaping over a river) have been down here in the Delta at least six months. Most of them have been on thirty or forty operations. Listen to them. They can save your life."

PFC Compella stares at Haney but his eyes don't see him. He is trying to sort through the few pieces of advice he remembers: "A sergeant tells you to get out of your hole you *get* out of your hole. He tells you lay down a base of fire you lay down a base of fire. He tells you to get your ass in gear and move across that open area toward that woodline, you move out. Yeah, you keep your eyes open and keep your weapon ready to fire, but you move out." And Haney: "Listen to your officers and NCO's. They can save your life." But how is that saving your life when they tell you to move toward a woodline full of VC? That must be where the man on either side of me gets it. He looks at Provenzano, then back at Haney.

"This is a strange war down here. We move around a lot. You don't know where you're going, when the MRB's going to shift anchorages, even when you're going out. We could go out tonight: you could be in a tango boat less than twelve hours from now, going into combat. Or we might go out in three days. The point is that you've got to learn fast. Alright.

"Forget about the tango boats and the so-called beach assaults. We'll talk about that later. Let's assume whatever platoon you're assigned to has gotten off the boat, is saddled up, and is moving out across open country. Down here that means mainly rice paddy, and at this time of year the paddies are starting to fill up again. Movement is slow and you get tired fast. It's hot as hell. How many of you people are sleepy right now?" Almost everyone raises a hand. "Alright, you're sleepy now, sitting on the deck of this rust-bucket doing nothing. Think what you're going to feel like after three hours' sleep on the third or fourth day of an operation, moving across open country in the sun. You're gonna be tired. You're gonna be thinking about the ship, or about R and R. You'll maybe have your weapon on your shoulder or you'll be lighting a cigarette. Or you're talking to your buddy. You'll lose your interval—say, you're moving in a line of skirmishers,

142

supposed to be ten meters apart, let's say. Somebody tells you you're backloading in an hour at some river a couple of clicks ahead . . ."

Haney slams the back of his right hand into the palm of his left, hard. "Bam, that's when Charlie opens up, and that's when you're most likely to get hit, when you're tired and when you think you got it made. If you're half-asleep maybe the people on point are half-asleep. They walk right into a treeline, right into the middle of a VC company. What does the VC company do? They don't do anything. They let the point keep going, right by them, and they wait 'til you're 150 meters away, or less. Then they open up on you.

"We rotate point in this company and if the people on point don't do their job—and it happens—you've got to be absolutely alert the whole time.

"OK. Say a company-minus is moving across a rice paddy in line and it takes some fire. What do you do?"

Bromleo, loud. "You heard the Lieutenant, whaddya do? Use your head!"

A Spec Four with a southern accent guesses: "Doesn't the company have an SOP?"

Haney and Bromleo look at each other, Haney smiling.

"The company does have an SOP," he says. "What would be an intelligent SOP in a case like that?"

The Spec Four: "Well, it would depend where you're taking the fire *from*. Say you were enfiladed from the left you might have the left four or five people lay down a base of fire and the rest of the unit—depending on how big it was, in this case, say, a platoon, try to

143

swing around and take the VC in the flank. That sort of thing. I suppose the main thing is to get as much fire on the suspected location as quick as possible."

Haney: "Good answer. Where'd you come from?"

"Americal Division. In-country transfer."

"Where're you from?"

"Charleston."

Haney looks him over. The inevitable southern solid citizen: cool, sure of himself, steady. Knows more about war by intuition than everything Haney has learned from experience or out of books.

"You ever carry a PRC-25?"

"Yes, Sir."

"My RTO got killed last week. You're the new one."

The others regard this as a mark of favor and they crane their heads around to look at him. They don't notice First Sergeant Bromleo, leaning against the railing of the ship with his arms folded across his chest. Just for a second he brings his lips together and shakes his head back and forth. Lieutenant Haney's RTO. This one'll last maybe a month if he's lucky.

In fact he has about twenty hours to live.

On the aft edge of the small flight deck of the *Samson* Colonel Robertson and Major Claiborn lean over the railing smoking, looking on unobserved at the troop-briefing going on below.

"Mind if I ask you a personal question, Sir?"

"Certainly I mind. I've got a lot to hide, Charles."

"Seriously. What do you think of the war?"

"Seriously. I know little of the larger issues and I

dislike what I know. I'm diffident on generalizations anyway."

"Diffident?" Claiborn isn't sure of the word.

Robertson shrugs. "Uncertain. The issues are tangled. Nothing's clear. I suppose you think they are."

"You saw what they did during TET."

"You saw what *we* did during TET."

"It's not the same thing."

"In any case it doesn't particularly bear on how we got involved."

"You think it's a civil war?"

"It is and it isn't."

"You like what you're doing? You like commanding a brigade?"

"Certainly. You get older, the options shrink in number. You're what, Charles? Thirty-four? You're beginning to get caught up in what I'm talking about. In a way it's like a lousy football game between two teams with lousy quarterbacks. You're in the bleachers. Nothing happens for three periods. You decide, the hell with it, I'll leave. But by that time there's a traffic jam outside. So you say, the hell with it, I'll stay. Then maybe your interest picks up, you start to think your being in the crowd yelling can influence what happens on the field . . ."

"We're *on* the field, Sir." There is a patronizing edge in Claiborn's voice.

"We are and we aren't. Put it this way. We're on the field and they're sending in the plays. But if we don't like what they're sending in . . ."

"This morning, for instance."

"OK, this morning. We don't play ball, Lemming sends in a new quarterback. You've had it done to you."

"Yes, Sir."

"You see what I mean."

"You think you'll get a star out of this?"

"Shit."

"Lemming fucks over you, doesn't he?"

"That's his way."

"You like his way?"

"What do you think?"

"Yeah. I suppose he'll get a third star."

"Without question. He'll be a lieutenant general within two months. They'll give it to him as soon as he leaves the Division."

"And then maybe Chief of Staff."

"Jesus."

"What don't you like about him?"

"You know Pope the poet?"

"No, Sir."

" 'Climbers, sir, assume the same position as creepers,' he said." Robertson points down at the new arrivals being briefed by Lieutenant Haney. "See those kids down there, listening to that lieutenant? They're wonderful kids. Six months ago they were taking cars apart, writing papers on Bret Harte. Now they're here, most of them don't know why or don't have the brains to sort out the issues. A lot of them are going to get killed, hosed down no questions asked. They come over here, they're not soldiers, and it rains on them or their buddy gets shot and suddenly they fight like tigers—

brave, selfless—as good as anybody who fought in Korea or Europe. Maybe better. They're the ones who go out and do it; them and Haney, that lieutenant. You and I, we get a round in the C and C if we're unlucky. Those kids are Willy and Joe, is what they are. They're not marines or airborne, they're Willy and Joe, only younger.

"And Lemming couldn't care less about them. That's fundamentally what I don't like about him. The farther up the line these bastards go, the less they think about where they've been, where *they* were thirty, forty years ago. I suppose the word for what he hasn't got is compassion. That's a word he doesn't even know the meaning of. Whaddayou think a general with compassion or a sense of justice would have told the Admiral, COMNAVFORV, this morning, when the Admiral told him about the Secretary of the Navy coming down here? The Admiral said to him, how about no helicopters, we got Mr. Ignatius going down to the Delta. Lemming lets it go by. Can't go to the barricades on a little thing like that. So now we're going into Kien Hoa again, two battalions riverine. You know what's going to happen."

"That won't happen," Claiborn says. "The 317th's in I Corps by now." He is uncomfortable listening to the Colonel go on like this. But Robertson continues:

"Whatever happens. It's a contemptible decision."

"Can't you argue with the General?"

"Yeah, I argue with him, blow the whistle on him. Then what?"

"You get the sack."

"I get the sack. The new quarterback doesn't blow the whistle."

Claiborn remains silent. What is there to say?

"You were in there this morning. You know what it's like arguing with him. Pointless. I know what you're thinking, too, Charles: you're going to soldier and soldier well and you're going to be a big general. Then you're going to change it. No more Lemmings will make it in your Army, right?"

"It can't be that bad."

"Keep believing it."

It has gone on long enough. Robertson changes the subject.

"When did the warning orders go out to the battalions?"

"Knapp sent them out last night. Then he countermanded them, after that scene in the study. He'd figured you'd just postpone the operation."

"Pretty cheeky thing for young man Knapp to do."

"Roger that. But it's been taken care of. I sent out new ones, talked to the '3's. The operations orders are redone; it's schemed for riverine. We'll have the regular back-brief this afternoon, launch on schedule from Thoi Son."

"You're an efficient little bastard, aren't you, Claiborn?"

"Like you say. Once more unto the breach."

"Airborne to you, Sir."

Below them Lieutenant Haney is finishing his lecture

on tactics, and the troops are stretching and walking back to the troop compartments. There is a distant scraping rumble as the *Samson's* anchor chain is winched into the ship. Within the half-hour the *Samson* and its sister ships—*Windham County, Delmore County, fitzClerk, Findon*—and all the hundred-odd riverine craft of the Mobile Riverine Force will be sweeping eastward down the Song My Tho toward the new anchorage.

"My briefing alright, First Sergeant?"

"Good, Lieutenant. Real good. You got 'em a little shook."

"That's the idea. Just a skosh bit shook. You know when they're going out for the first time?"

"Yes, Sir. Tonight. About 0300 I figure."

"How'd you know that? I found out on my way down here."

" 'Look at the man on either side of you.' That business."

"Yeah. Well, you know what to do."

★ 16 ★

Riverine Boat Convoy
en route, Thoi Son Anchorage
to Objective
0445, 14 March 1968

INSIDE the ATC all is blackness and settled heat. Ignoring the low-slung steel seats fitted to the deck and placed along the bulkheads like seats on a bus, the soldiers of Compella's platoon sprawl on their backs or curl up like children on the deck, their radios, helmets, and packs as pillows. "You sit on the seats and the boat hits a mine, you won't get shrapnel up your ass. The seat could save your life." But so can the flak-vests some of the troops are lying on, they rationalize; besides, the 1st Platoon's tango boat is fourth in the line-ahead convoy: it won't trigger any mines. Lying down, the troops are just below the waterline, four feet of armor plating above them on either side.

The convoy throbs slowly ahead. But for the regular muted rhythms of the engine and the hissing of the sternwash it is utterly still. Paul Compella lies on his back and looks up through a hole in the canvas overhead. He is quite comfortable, and like most of the young odds-players who fight in this war, more relaxed than he had imagined he would be. For soldiers going out on their first combat mission it is difficult to distinguish between bravado and confidence, and because it is reassuring to think the young veterans with whom they serve are confident, they come to believe it. Thus the gestures, the laconic remarks, the ribaldries of the veterans signify the absence of real and immediate danger. The Los Angeles freeway is worse than this, they insist absently, and then look over at their friends, standing on the AMMI pontoons, waiting to board the tango boats. " 'Scuse me, Compella. Hey, Mike, I got a Jacqueline Susann. You got *The Carpetbaggers?* Shit, I got some real skin, *Night in a Moorish Harem.* How many cigarettes you bring? Four packs, an optimist, huh? We'll be out a lot longer than that."

Camouflage discipline: a mockery. The veterans have enough crap stuck in their helmet-bands to start a drugstore: insect repellent, cigarettes, matches, paperbacks, ballpoints. Bromleo, wandering among them, says nothing.

Four times out of five, it's a walk in the woods.

Aboard ship Compella had showered and put on fresh fatigues, had poured talcum powder down the front of his chest. He feels clean, dry, fresh. Every ten or fifteen seconds a fleck of spray lights on his face, dries to salt. What was that thing the priest has, that he throws, sprinkles water on corpses with? A kind of

151

salt-shaker with a handle he shakes at you before the pall-bearers throw their gloves in? Compella pulls back a hand another soldier has started to roll over on, puts it by his side; the other hand, left side. More flecks of spume, gentle, almost imperceptible.

On wet days the open graves of funerals have awnings over them. And if a corpse could see, it would see what Compella sees now, looking up, black barely shading to deep green. And if it could feel, it would feel what he feels, the ground underneath and on either side barely trembling with the shifting of weight by the mourners, one foot to the other, just as the boat trembles with the stresses of engine throb and river current. People with some stake in your life, friends some of them, people who sense an obligation to attend, they would be there, standing all around, worried about how the anguish or grief projects on their faces. For most of the mourners the connection with him would be slight, even impersonal: a connection like that with the sailors in the aft-turret, their whispers now audible.

The river slides underneath like lava sliding down a mountain of glass. The troops shift in their dozing, rearrange their bodies. Again the scene settles in Compella's mind, the suggestions multiply. It would be a revenge, he decides: Carol there, not of the family, so standing back, unveiled, regretting her disaffection, her babbling about creative radicalization and nay-plam. Who would she go out with? The candidate at Newport in his whites? But she would never forget him in her lifetime, Compella thinks. And his mother, close up, sobbing quietly, drily. Father, proud: standing erect in his tears. Sisters perhaps not in control. The teams. Teachers, sportswriters, construction men who drove him around as a small boy.

Two or three stars appear in the opening in the canvas above, and the blackness is perhaps less intense. Toward the stern of the well-deck three soldiers, stretched on their sides, prop themselves on their elbows and talk quietly. Their bodies lean slightly, in a synchronized easy movement, and the steely creaks of the boat suggest it is turning south, down off the My Tho into the Giao Thong. In their dozing men seem to sense the turn, to apprehend the closeness of the beaches, now but an hour ahead.

The convoy moves in line down the Giao Thong.

The water is warm, bouillon-textured, lifting Compella toward the mirror of the surface. He somehow wills the arrest of his slow tumbling, resists the lift, pulling dully forward by sweeping his arms in arcs toward his sides. In this suspended state he feels neither instinct nor urge to breathe; only the desperate necessity of resolving his disorientation by touch, by clutch: anything—vines, roots, branches. He cannot see the bottom. An overwhelming pressure, not yet pain, forces against the nape of his neck, pressing him down again, slowing his progress forward. And all at once the pain overwhelms him and he is out of air. Pulling forward again, he looks above, sees through the dark orange of the water the leg that got his neck, sees it frogleg and dangle. He follows it, reaches out, grasps a branch, surfaces.

Blessedly he has come up under the overhanging

jungle along the bank, and the machine gun which had direct fire into the tango boat when its ramp dropped, fifteen feet from the "beach," cannot reach him. Now it appears the boat has begun backing down, almost as though the .50-cal bullets playing along its bulkhead are moving it. But it is dead in the water. Compella cannot tell from where he is how many are still aboard, how many have thrown themselves into the river.

Three or four feet behind him, on a direct line between him and the boat, a body floats without motion like a body-surfer's without waves. One wrist is laid over the other, and the hands of the body hang limp before it. Anchored by the crook of his elbow Compella reaches to secure the swimmer, his weapon hanging off his right arm.

"Leave him alone, you. You'll get your arm shot off."

First Sergeant Bromleo is suddenly next to him, panting like an old bellows but calm. "Leave him alone. I got people're gonna get that fuckin' gun. Stay right where you are, you got that?" Compella shakes his head. "You alright, Private?" Bromleo adds, but, not waiting for an answer, breast-strokes away from him, under the overhang. By resting the side of his face against the water, leaning out from the bank, Compella can see that the floating body is now in direct line with a small clearing, a kind of grassy sluice that is the machine-gun's field of fire from its bunker.

The gun spatters again, still trained on the boat, and the body floats by degrees away from him. Compella leans back in, shifts, suspends himself by both hands from branches above him, wondering how long the machine gun can keep it up. Or how long it will take them to get to it. Around him the smoke and shouting and stuttering of fires dissipate slowly, and he begins to take stock. The remnants of the platoon, those who have made it to the south bank of the river, are strung out at irregular intervals, all pressed into the bank and clutching. Bromleo's orders to them all are the same. "Stay where you are; I got people're gonna get that gun."

The tango boats that had followed Compella's in the convoy have veered toward midstream, away from the helpless ATC, playing their .50's and cannon onto the bank above the platoon. The remainder of the battalion, still aboard the boats, is moving upstream toward the farther beach areas.

It is some minutes until the bunker is destroyed and the VC machine gun silenced. But almost immediately Bromleo appears again alongside him: "OK OK, they're out of there. Get your ass on the bank and follow Logan." Compella moves toward the opening in the deadfall, porpoises himself onto it, and runs at a crouch along the cleared plane of fire. The bunker, a mud carapace with logged sides, is ten meters inland; behind it is a small clearing now filling up with the 1st Platoon.

"I got this place secured," Lieutenant Haney announces, standing in the clearing. "People around the clearing. You guys coming out of the river check your weapons and ammo. I hope to Christ you haven't lost them in the river. We're not gonna stay here long."

The troops fling themselves to the ground. Of the

thirty people on the boat—including Haney and the Company First Sergeant—sixteen are in the clearing, several of them walking wounded. Four others are out around the position as security. Ten are missing: still on the boat, dead, wounded, or unhurt, or drowned or dead in the water. The clearing is 200 meters from its assigned landing site farther up the Rach Ba Nho, for the moment useless to anyone.

And there the platoon remains for some hours, by-passed by the remainder of the battalion going ashore upriver, placed in reserve by the company commander. Later, when the "seal" is established, room will be found for it on the battalion line finally deployed between the two rivers.

Battle histories often project a certain luminosity and logic. They are worked up from a variety of sources: interviews, map studies, combat after-action reports, newspaper articles, captured documents, and talking prisoners. The same logic, the same reduction to order, invariably characterizes the higher commanders' understanding of the battle they are trying to direct. And as the outlines of a battle in progress become in some sense intelligible to the commanders higher up, the details, the individual agonies, become blurred and merged in what they call the "overview." The private hells of death and drowning and being wounded must be borne, in this case, by the soldiers of the 1st Platoon, Company "A", 1st Battalion, 71st Infantry. Their ecstasies of terror, their small acts of courage and compassion can be shared by no one but Haney and Bromleo. But the situation reports of the Lieutenant and the Sergeant translate on the radio nets as curt comments, demands for fires, reports of wounded.

Lieutenant Colonel Plowman, overhead in his small command chopper, listens, gives advice, encouragement, makes promises, factors out the inessential, renders reports to Robertson and Claiborn, for the moment at their command boat at Fire Base BRADLEY. Thus: "Part of my "A" Company is in trouble. One boat shot up. Remainder of battalion safely ashore and maneuvering to destroy enemy positions on BLUE Beach I."

To which George Robertson replies, "Roger. You have casualty estimate?"

To which Plowman, "Negative as to specifics. Estimate twenty friendly KIA or WIA."

To which Robertson, "Roger, out."

Thus Robertson, as always in complete (to the others exasperatingly complete) control of himself, has utterly no control over the particularities of the fighting, and very little influence over the general implementing of Captain Knapp's plan (now revised to allow for the absence of helicopters).

Notwithstanding, the general outline of the battle soon becomes discernible, the outline of a continent seen on a large-scale map from across the room. Robertson's two battalions sailed into the objective area. The first of these got ashore with some trouble—part of its "A" Company ambushed in a boat, sustaining moderate casualties. But the other companies made good their landings upriver; and, being landed, swung around, eliminated the VC direct fire weapons pinning down part of "A" Company. Then they fanned out between the two rivers, and soon were deployed in line across the inland peninsula, facing west. Meantime, Robertson's 2nd Battalion landed unopposed at Beaches BLACK 1, 2, and 3: the VC's attention had been riveted on the 1st. By the time the enemy had realized that this second battalion had gone ashore in their "rear," it was too late for them to escape in order to the west, though small parties made it through. But by noon the second battalion was also in line, facing the other, 2000 meters between them; most of the VC were in the middle, and the airstrikes were beginning to come in on them.

All of this Robertson apprehended by noon, 14 March. All these general outlines.

★ 17 ★

"THEY'RE sealed in there."

"Yeah, sealed. Who the fuck told you that?"

"I heard it. I heard Lieutenant Haney say Colonel Plowman told the CO the whole battalion's sealed in there."

"Come on. Compella, you know what it takes to seal a VC battalion in a place like that?"

"Whip it on me."

"How 'bout a lead fence twenty feet high with a cement foundation ten feet deep. With no breaks. Maybe one division U.S. standing on top of the fence, each man with an M-60."

"What about the rivers? How'd they get across them at night? We got thirty, forty boats in the rivers."

"If they want to, if they're even in there, they'll get out."

159

But the prognosis, as Major Claiborn reads it, remains good. Robertson agrees with him. It is 2300. The three exhausted companies of the 1st Battalion are on line, "A" Company's right "anchored" (as the after-action report will describe it) on the Rach Ba Nho, its left positions tied in with Bravo Company, whose left in turn is Charlie Company's right. This last unit's night positions stretch directly south to the north bank of the Song Sao. The aggregate is about 350 troops, subtracting the losses of the morning's ambushes and subsequent fire fights. The battalion holds the eastern side of the "seal," river to river, a distance of 1000 meters.

Two kilometers to the west, the 2nd of the 71st is likewise on line, stretched bank to bank, facing the 1st Battalion. Its casualties are negligible—six wounded —but if there is an attempt at a break-out, they will have to stop it. The two rivers are cluttered with boats: ASPB's, Monitors, ATC's, the revving of their engines as they back down or lumber out of each other's way suggesting a huge sportscar rally. From Claiborn's present vantage point, from the grease-penciled mapsheet propped against the bulkhead of the CCB, it does indeed appear that the VC are "sealed." Yes, some will get out, men who can hold their breath a long time, he reflects with a shrug, a few small parties of desperate confused soldiers who will crawl through the deadfall, get through the 2nd Battalion's line and exfiltrate to the west; but no more than these. How can they? "If I was COSVN I'd relieve his ass," he says quietly, thinking of the VC commander. "If you're lucky, they won't have to," somebody says.

Gunships have been overhead, off and on, for almost an hour. The two 105 batteries at BRADLEY have been shooting into the encirclement since 2130, halting their fires only when the gunships come over. There is even a chance a 155 battery can make it to Cao Sang by daylight. That would really do it. And all the while, the gunboats, cruising in a miniature parody of "line ahead," have been throwing everything—cannon, .50's, .30 cal, into the objective area. It is impossible that the 317th can survive.

Horne, Logan, and Compella share a position on "A" Company's extreme right, barely ten meters from the Rach Ba Nho. They are all that remain of their squad. And they have just begun thinking they've got it made. Relieved and exhausted, they are pleased to follow Lieutenant Haney's curt orders: "Anything you see moving in front of you, any sound in the river past your position, shoot it. Otherwise stay where you are. No more than one man sleeps at a time. For Christsake don't shoot unless you've got something to shoot at."

There it is. Logan dully remembers a briefing map. "They'll never try it out this side." The night is hot and dark and stinking. Horne, his head against Compella's thigh, sleeps deeply. Compella has been lying on his belly for an hour now, behind an M-60, its barrel propped over a log. Logan stares through the clutter of vines and deadfall at the open space that is the river. Directly to Compella's front, perhaps 400 meters into the bush, the supposed positions of the VC remain targets for every support weapon the MRF disposes.

The scene, hazy and recessed, more visible to the

imagination than sight, gives no clues about the enemy. The flares disappear, and it is black again. Over the 1st Battalion's positions, perhaps 400 feet up, a gunship bats through the air, back and forth. Compella tries to guess its position, looks up through the skeletal gaps in the canopy, sees nothing. Suddenly, however, a stream of what looks like solid tracer escapes the gunship, molten pink, its hot liquid shaft probing the inside of the encirclement. The gun makes a brooding sound like the hum of a dentist's drill from the waiting-room. And the shaft seems to probe like a drill, each pitchless burst a question curtly phrased: Are you there? Do you feel? And when the question has been asked, and no answer given, it poses its question in a slightly different idiom, in a new tone, getting at the hidden targets from new angles. Suddenly the shaft touches a nerve. The patient screams for an instant, regains his composure. Compella and Logan can only guess where he is. Apparently satisfied, the shaft disappears groundward. Still the 105's do not fire; save for the boat noises and the invisible slapping of the gunship rotor it is silent again.

Again. Refreshed, the dentist having selected a new drillhead, the engine returns to work, the pink shaft angling down, probing once more, this time from a point immediately over Compella. He has a sudden recollection of Dr. Gray back in Torrington, a calm man who talks baseball when he walks over to the sideboard to get a new drillhead: "Malzone is a complete third baseman, hits for power, guns his throws like a cannon, steadies the pitchers down. OK, Paul, open up again, huh?" "Is this the last drill?" "No, second to the last; it may hurt, I'm close to a nerve." And the fiery small hum preens itself again in the back of his mouth. "He hit one out of Fenway Sunday that went over *every*thing, green monster, screen, everything." Paul's fingers tighten around the ends of the chair-arms, the drill stops. Dr. Gray walks over for another drillhead, the last one: "That was no Fenway home run."

The gunship, still overhead, still unsatisfied, probes again, asking its questions at length now, less patiently. The shaft flickers down, becomes solid, more intense. Suddenly the gunship is Compella, Sr., standing at his boy's back, coldly angry, speaking invective to an older boy who has just slapped his son. The father has taken up the argument, and having resolved it, disappears.

His son squiggles, changing position, looks over at Logan. "Look at that shit. You hear what Haney said, a mini-gun like that, on a chopper at 500 feet, could put a round in every square foot of the Ann Arbor stadium in thirty seconds."

"Keep your voice down. That's no fuckin' mini-gun. There's no bunkers in the stadium."

"Whatever it is."

Again the gunship, this time farther away. It spits another long pinkness, the longest one yet, still refusing to acknowledge its failures. Finally it stops altogether, the shaft at last announcing its resignation in driblets. The gunship moves out of hearing.

A flare pops softly over the encirclement, and again

the landscape defines itself in a flash, the light fading bright to hazy ochre. Through the cluttered skeletons of burnt trees Compella stares, ignoring the night-vision warnings. But still there is no movement. What do they do, he wonders, just lie there? Why don't their wounded cry out? They must be dug in, but if their bunkers along the river were that good they couldn't have spent much time preparing bunkers where they are now. No way. They can't tunnel in there; two feet down it's water. All they can do is scrape and burrow, pressing their faces to the mud, hoping it's the man on either side of them.

The flare has signaled a new inning for the artillery, and Compella hears the reports of the guns at BRAD-LEY, waits, waits, the rounds at last searing through overhead, rushing down. The earth shakes with the blasts and seconds later, like rain on metal, the spent shrapnel slaps the broken canopy overhead. The explosions seem without definition, monstrously compressed roars. The whole sequence begins to repeat itself, again, irregular but without letting up—a distant guttural sound, silence, a sucking rush overhead, the blast and shock in front, metal on palm-frond, shards falling around them.

Logan and Compella lie facing each other, heads up against the log, pressed close to the ground. The artillery barrages begin to roll forward, away from their position toward the western part of the encirclement.

"Compella," Logan whispers, "Were you at Division before you came down here?"

"For two days."

"What's it like?"

"Whaddya mean, what's it like?"

"Ever see the General?"

"Yeah, I saw him. I saw him one morning in a briefing."

"Did he say anything?"

"He just asks questions and listens. He doesn't say anything."

"I mean, what does he do?"

"He runs the Division, whaddya mean, what does he do?"

"Like, just shouts at people and they run around and do it, like that? Do they get incoming at Division?"

"Once in a while. You were at the Young Lion Academy."

"The Young Lion Academy. What kinda shit is that? The Young Lion Academy. They brainwash your ass. The Young Lion Academy. They try to make the whole thing a big game, like a joust, all that shit. Like the Rams with those horns on their helmet, you know, in football, all that halftime jazz. Biggest bass drum in the universe. Everybody prancing around, then they go out and get their ligaments torn to shit and their collarbones broken."

"You're a cynic, Logan."

"Keep your voice down."

Compella senses movement in front of their positions, like a tiny stirring of water.

"Y'hear that?"

"Yeah, maybe it'll rain."

"I thought it didn't rain at night."

"Sometimes it does," Logan answers, "God gets pissed off."

"You're a cynic, Logan."

"Shit."

The gunship returns again and begins reworking the VC battalion.

Major Claiborn and Lieutenant Colonel Plowman are orchestrating from within the CCB, manning the radio consoles in the well-deck. They shift from one net to another with practiced ease, secure and comforted in their expertise. They coordinate the fires of boats, gunships, artillery; record SITREPS from the company command posts, trying to evoke a clear picture of the night battle. Robertson studies them from his field-table, drinking his coffee out of a canteen cup. He sifts through the grating fogs of static, taking in the transmissions, rarely speaking, hearing the shower falling on the overhead.

He can abide most ambiguities, but this one is different. There is a VC battalion not five clicks away, a ragged unit pounded and churned into mud. There can be little exfiltration tonight, so the odds are good that his brigade can sweep through in the morning, collect the weapons, and count the bodies. The battle has cost the brigade a certain price, as always a terrible price, but not as terrible as he had promised General Lemming. The friendly casualties will be "moderate" ones on the after-action reports, moderate enough for Lemming to claim a significant victory. The point was, he considers, that the absent helicopter company could

have reduced them almost to nothing, could have kept
Colonel Plowman's "A" Company out of the boat ambush. However.

Moths and bugs clog the tiny bulb overhead. The
light is bleak, dreary. The Colonel clasps his hands
behind his head, leans back, listening, remembering . . .

> Western wind, when wilt thou blow
>> The small rain down can rain?
> Christ, if my love were in my arms,
>> And I in my bed again . . .

and says: "What's it look like, Plowman?"

"Beautiful. Best night operation I ever saw."

"Good."

To Compella's right, 100 meters in front of the position, a .50 cal on board a Monitor fires into the north
side, the river side of the seal, hoarse popping blasts
of five or six rounds each, a short break between
fusillades while the gun traverses. The tide is in, so
that the gunboat has direct fire into the VC, doesn't
have to worry about wasting ammo on the riverbank.
All the same, it does little but reassure the Americans
on line at either end; the VC are not in the habit of
walking around in their night positions when taking
fire. The Monitor keeps it up for five or six minutes,
firing into the blackness and the rain.

Some of the night sounds don't fit the pattern.
Compella shifts back onto his stomach, lifts up on his
elbows, slowly, his eyes rising just above the top of
the log. He drags the stock of the M-60 tight into his
shoulder, sighting on nothing, squeezing, squeezing the

hand-guard and the narrow part of the stock like a baseball bat.

"Hey, Logan? How 'bout that? Y'hear that?"

"No," Logan whispers. "I told you, they're not gonna come through here. Maybe the river, along the bank, but not in front of us."

But if they did, Compella wonders to himself, if they did, could we hear them? He remembers a drill sergeant at Polk. "For example, during the Korean War. The Chinese would blow bugles or play records on loudspeakers, right in the middle of night. This was the way these people had of trying to demoralize an opponent, trying to scare the hell out of him by making him think there were large numbers of Reds. The Japs would do the same kind of thing, like in the John Wayne movies: 'Marine, you die.' This is what you call a crude form of psychological warfare, and it didn't shake our people up in 1944 or 1952, any more than if the VC did it it would shake you up now. What you know you're not afraid of. But the VC don't do that. Those people are smart as hell. They've been playing their little game a long time. You down there in nametape defilade, you asleep, just like you'll be some night in a NDP and Charlie'll zap your ass." The soldier in Compella's basic training company was sitting in the second row of the grandstand at Fort Polk, getting his night indoctrination. He was falling asleep in the warm dusk, and, staring at the ground, was trying to strike an impression of rapt, musing concentration. "You don't look at the ground, you look at me! Needle-dick Nick the bug-fucker, aren't you, Private? You're gonna go to sleep in Vietnam, aren't you? Ain't gonna be any bugles in Vietnam, you better listen up at night, you got me? You listen for every fucking rustle in the night . . ."

But as the night wears on in Kien Hoa, in the lulls of shelling and aerial machine-gunning, the rustles of the night merge in a sibilant unvarying regularity. Compella, anyone, can only react to the promptings of his imagination, unless the VC were to get desperate, and being desperate reveal themselves. In which case, hell, he's got nothing to worry about. Logan said it: they'd never come through here.

"I wish we had a starlight scope."

"They're all in the drink. Got shot down. Three hundred dollars apiece, twenty-four of them. They went down in a chopper. They won't come through here."

In a starlight scope you saw the enemy moving as you saw men moving on the bank if you were under water, through an amber haze. Then you lost sight, surfaced, made the bank, found yourself unhurt, and being unhurt when others were dying, felt a terrible exhilaration. I made it through that, I made it through that, Compella thinks, and when the morning comes I will have made it through the whole thing. A soft gravelly sound to his right; Horne turns over in his sleep. "They won't come through here."

"The fuck they wouldn't!" Compella is up on his knees, screaming like a savage. He cocks the gun desperately and fires a long stuttering burst into the clearing up ahead. Logan rolls up, slams the M-79 shut, fires too, drops beside Compella to help feed the M-60. Out of the haze a dark rush of figures comes toward them, one stumbling, another pitching forward on its face. A third, only a charging outline, detaches itself from the cluster, skids sharply to Compella's right front, regains its balance, skitters toward the riverbank in a crouch. Jarred awake, Horne grabs in the wet for his M-16, and, reaching it, crumples without a sound. Compella can only keep firing at the dissolving forms still in front, moving toward them. He dimly senses Logan has gone after Horne's weapon, is firing toward the river.

All the forces resist, as in a dream. The moment lengthens to hours, the expectation of completion and safety somehow undergirding everything as it happens. The gun responds, but somehow distantly, as if fired by itself; the after-images of the scrambling forms remain. But are they people, are they still there?

A long burst off to the right, splattering into the river. Logan is dealing with the VC in the undergrowth along the bank, the VC now sinking into the bush, maybe dead, maybe wounded, perhaps already in the water. He is back alongside Compella, brushing against him. "Jesus," he says, but not loud, not scared, just the word. He feeds Compella's gun, firing now at nothing. At there. It stops. A cloud of silence settles closely about them.

"You get that guy in the river, Logan?"

But Logan did not get the VC flying toward the river, and suddenly, a scarlet viscous bubble created from nothing, there wells up in Paul Compella's skull the agony of a death wound, exploding as from within, pushing and blasting out with a terrible force. A long sliver of bone, rent up and out through flesh, plops across Compella's right eye, its end stuck to the wound like a hangnail. "Logan," he says, and crumples onto the log.

"The fuck was that?" Haney is alongside Logan, more angry, it sounds, than concerned. Like the others he has not expected VC probes on the east side of the seal. Jarred out of his dozing he has crawled forward to Compella's position.

"I said what the hell was that?"

Logan, shaking, nudges his shoulder and points at Horne and Compella. "They tried to come through here. Horne's dead. Compella's breathing. Look at his face . . ."

"Alright, we'll get him out of here. Hang on. You alright?"

"I'm alright."

"Give me the radio."

"Cheetah 6, this is 3."

"This is 6. Whatcha got?"

"3. We got one KIA, one bad WIA, over."

"Roger that. What's your situation?"

"3. They tried to come through my right, along the river. Nothing now."

"How many, Logan?" Haney asks.

"Four, Sir, four or five."

"Four or five, 6."

"Roger. You got VC KIA on the position? Over."

"Negative, none I can see. Wait." He looks at Logan,

who shakes his head. "Man on the position says un-known."

"This is 6, ah, get the WIA out. My position twenty meters from route GREEN. We got a boat here. What is condition of WIA? Over."

"3. Critical, repeat critical. Will get him out, over."

"6. Try to confirm enemy KIA, over."

"Negative at this time. WIA is Compella, PFC, joined unit yesterday. Out." And to Logan. "Joined the unit yesterday, right?"

"Yes, Sir, joined the unit a couple days ago . . ."

☆ 18 ☆

Command Boat
Kinh Giao Thong, Kien Hoa Province
0030, 15 March 1968

ON the CCB, now tied up on the west bank of the
Giao Thong about 1000 meters behind the 1st Battalion
positions, Robertson senses the rain has stopped. He
reaches out, clutches Lieutenant Colonel Plowman by
the elbow.

"What's your casualty situation right now?"

"Unchanged from 1800, far as I know, Sir. Last I
have is sixteen KIA, sixty wounded. Bad. Not as bad
as I thought; most of the wounded aren't serious.
What's the story on 2/71?"

"Six wounded, very light. You went in first, you were
the bait, I guess. The VC went after you. Probably
cleared their positions on the south river as soon as
they heard the ambushes on the Rach Ba Nho this
morning. Your people got it again, more than they
could handle, more than they deserved."

173

"Not more than we could handle, Sir," Plowman says gently, a little truculence in his voice. "We'll do it again if we have to."

"You did fine, Jim, you know that," Robertson says quietly, reading the bone-weariness in his face. "Get some sleep, flop on the mattress over there. We have any trouble tonight it's not going to be your people."

"I will. Thank you, Sir." He walks over and sinks onto the mattress.

Claiborn and Robertson look at each other, both shaking their heads.

"Tiger 6, Cheetah 6, over."

Major Claiborn answers for Plowman. "Roger, Cheetah."

"Cheetah 6. VC probe on my right at zero-zero one-five. I got one KIA, one WIA. No further enemy activity. Am evacuating US WIA by riverine."

"Roger, Cheetah. Out." Claiborn turns around abruptly, staring at Robertson: "Should I wake up Colonel Plowman?"

"No. Don't wake him up. Let him sleep."

It was a good encirclement. The 1st Brigade had stolen a leaf from Colonel Morton's book. At 0220 the 155's registered, honed in on the enemy position, began pounding away. With textbook synchronization the other support fires were registered, locked in, fired, lifted. The gunships returned four more times during the night. The monitors on either river kept up their shelling almost without pause. At either end of the terrain pocket the two battalions slept, watched, waited for VC attempts to break out, wondering if the bastards were really still in the pocket. But in the sad pre-dawn grayness, the supporting fires lifted for the last time and the last flare fired; they understood that, at least, if the VC were still inside and alive, there would be no attempt to break out. At 0700 Colonel Robertson ordered his units to sweep toward each other and determine what the night of shelling had done to the 317th. He and Claiborn went up in the C and C to oversee the operation.

Preliminary body-counts and a complete absence of resistance indicating a more than substantial victory, he ordered the battalions to complete their sweep, backload, and return to the Mobile Riverine Base. Then he flew home to the *Samson.*

The results of MRF operation 18-68 were tersely summarized late on the afternoon of 15 March in a combat after-action report the industrious Knapp prepared for Robertson's approval. The report stated:

. . . helicopter assets being unavailable, the brigade-minus abandoned its original scheme of operation for search-and-clear missions in Cao Sang District, Kien Hoa Province. The targeted enemy unit remained the 317th Main Force Battalion.

As originally schemed, 2d Battalion, 71st Infantry, was to have conducted beach assaults on the south bank of the Mekong (Song My Tho), moved overland to a pick-up zone, there to await airmobile movement to a landing-zone immediately west of the objective area. From this landing-zone the battalion was to have deployed into blocking positions oriented east, thereby creating a seal anchored on the south bank of the Rach Ba Nho and the north bank of the Song Sao. First Battalion, 71st Infantry, was to have conducted beach assaults on sites on the north shore of the Rach Ba Nho, 200 meters west of its juncture with the Giao Thong; from here it would have swept west, toward the 2d battalion's block.

As noted, helicopter assets were denied, and the plan had to be changed. First battalion, 71st Infantry, landed at the sites originally selected for it at 0720 hours, 14 March. This landing was opposed. One ATC was crippled, losing power and unable to steer; the platoon aboard suffered heavy casualties, such as to render it combat ineffective for some hours. The remainder of the battalion made good its landings farther up the Rach Ba Nho. During this landing phase of the operation the battalion took 11 KIA and 31 WIA, the majority of those killed from the ambushed platoon.

. . . Second Battalion, 71st Infantry, meantime, had moved in riverine convoy down the Giao Thong, turning west onto the Song Sao. It was not ambushed. Its beach assaults were unopposed. By 1200 hours, 14 March, the companies of this battalion were in their assigned blocking positions and the seal was made. The battalion's casualties to this time were six wounded.

First Battalion, 71st Infantry, was deployed into its blocking position by 1230 hours. Supporting fires into the encirclement then intensified, continuing without substantial pause until approximately 0500 hours, 15

March. Enemy exfiltration was detected at one point only, on the extreme right of 1/71's block, the battalion sustaining one KIA and one WIA.

. . . At 0700 both battalions commenced to sweep through the objective area, completing their search at 1100. On orders of the brigade commander, the units then backloaded and returned to the MRB.

Preliminary estimates establish enemy losses as follows:

VC KIA, by BC	158
Hoi Chanh	2
VC captured	11
VC weapons captured	120 (110 indiv; 10 crew-svd)
Other	90 lbs. medical supplies
	15 lbs. documents

. . . Operation 18-68 must be accounted only a qualified success. The provision of helicopters, which would have enabled the brigade to proceed according to its original plan, would have minimized friendly casualties and enemy exfiltration.

For the Commander:

The report was taken to Colonel Robertson for his approval only after a long argument between an exhausted Major Claiborn and a fresh, outraged Captain Knapp. Good soldier that he was, the S-3 recognized the polemics were justified by what had happened. But combat after-action reports are not supposed to be polemics. They must recite the facts, and the facts only. Division knew that Robertson had tried, and failed, to get helicopter assets for his brigade; no sense tearing off the scabs of barely healed wounds by reminding Division of an old and acerbic controversy. Besides, it would probably mean Robertson's relief from command. General Lemming's decision to withhold a helicopter company hurt the brigade and the brave sailors who had carried it to the objective; on the other hand, the River Lions had achieved an exceptionally large body-count. Robertson's stock would rise automatically, if he kept his mouth shut. Lemming might listen to him next time around. Why jeopardize the prospect?

"Because, goddamit, I want it to be a matter of written record. Alright? Lemming's not going to put his arms around Colonel Robertson just because we killed a bunch of VC in one battle. Nothing's going to change."

Claiborn hasn't the heart to kill the report. "Alright, Knapp"—he stops drumming his fingers on the desk— "we'll take it to the Colonel."

★ 19 ★

U.S.S. *Samson, APB-58*
Thoi Son Anchorage
1700 Hours, 15 March 1968

CLAIBORN and Knapp find Colonel Robertson sitting alone in the immaculate study, watching the smoke of his cigar drift toward the open porthole. His hands are folded together, thumbs under his chin, elbows resting on the dining-table. From the pontoon below the distant murmur of the troops' conversation can be heard, but the punctuation of laughter and wisecracks is gone. They are standing in the gray haze drinking beer. In spite of his exhaustion—he has not slept for forty hours—Robertson appears calm and rested. He is uncharacteristically spruce in fresh jungle fatigues and clean-shaven. Without looking up he is aware of their entrance, and pointing at the Commodore's closed door, as if sensing the urgency of their visit, gestures for them to talk quietly.

Claiborn is solicitous: "Excuse me, Colonel. We're

sorry to bother you now. Knapp has written up the preliminary after-action report. I assume you've been in touch with General Lemming?"

Still staring at the porthole Robertson nods. "I've talked to the General. He was up at 2d Brigade all yesterday, but I called him this afternoon."

"Is he pleased?"

"Pleased. Is the General pleased. Does it please the General. Will't please you to rise, Sir? We'll meet the company below. Interesting way of putting it, Charles, is the General *pleased?*"

"You want us to come back later, Colonel?" Neither Claiborn or Knapp has ever seen the *gamin* in him; only heard about it.

"No, my friends, it pleases me that you should stay. You *do* wish to please your Colonel, do you not?" Still he does not look at them. They shift uneasily on their feet. Claiborn decides this is not an attractive side to the Colonel's character but writes it off as fatigue.

Robertson finally tears himself away from the play of motes, snaps out of himself. "Yes, Charles, the Great Man is pleased. I trust neither of you is preparing to upset him?" He suddenly turns toward them, staring archly.

"I can't say that, Sir. Captain Knapp has written up the combat after-action report. It has to go out on the C and C at 1800, or whenever the rain lets up. You want to look at it before it goes up? You should look at it, Colonel."

"I should look at it, huh, not to mention sign it?" Knapp hands it to him like a schoolboy handing a bad report card to his father. The Colonel puts on his half-rim tortoise shells, spins around on his chair, takes the report and studies it.

They strain to pick up his reactions to the controversial paragraphs, Knapp self-righteously hoping it will provoke arguments. But the Colonel finishes without a flicker of disapproval on his face and resumes staring out the porthole.

"You know, Knapp," he says finally, "when I heard you and the Major come in here I expected you were going to ask me a question. Not the one you asked, not ask me to read a report, but to ask me something no one's asked me since we went into Kien Hoa. An important question, too, one might even say the *only* question. You know what I'm thinking about?"

Claiborn and Knapp stare at each other. "No, Sir," Knapp replies, sorely disappointed in himself.

"You don't, huh? Your Colonel is not pleased." He turns back to them. "OK. We've played games long enough, afloat and ashore. How many'd we lose out there this time, Charles, sixteen killed, seventy-odd wounded, not counting the Navy?"

"Yes, Sir."

"I'm thinking about one of our friends in a high place, higher than General Lemming. I'm thinking of our distinguished visitor, the one allergic to helicopters, the one we went out again to prove the concept of riverine mobility for. You recollect now who I mean?"

"Jesus. He never came. The son of a bitch never came."

"No. He never came. Yesterday at 1400 he got in

a C-130 and flew up to Da Nang to decorate some marines. This afternoon he flies back to Washington." Robertson's voice is cold, without expression. "Only don't call him a son of a bitch. He doesn't know, probably will never know, what went on here yesterday in his behalf."

With a dramatic flourish Knapp flicks the ballpoint out of his fatigue-jacket pocket and hands it to George Robertson, who signs his name to the report. "Send it up to Division. Put an "Eyes Only" on it and address it to the General, not to G-3. Don't make any changes. Save a copy for me."

"Yes, Sir," Claiborn says.

"I can make it worse, Colonel." Knapp.

"No, send it as it is. Don't change a word." He looks out the porthole again and puffs on his cigar.

"Thank you, Colonel."

"Get out of here, both of you. Go have a beer. Get pleased."

5:30 P.M. The afternoon monsoon now buffets Kien Hoa Province and the Song My Tho. It is a great gray swirl, the waters coming down as if from huge sluices, warm sleet pelting the remnants of the 317th escaping to the south, and the U.S.S. Samson, buttoned up against the storm. It is like the desperate punishment of some frustrated God, Robertson reflects, hearing the rain against the skin of the ship. But the punishment, the daily afternoon scourge, is neither lengthened nor intensified from day to day. For almost a week the monsoon rains have come in the late afternoons; the dry season is finished. The rains will be a part of the 1st Brigade's operations for the next five months.

Most of which, Robertson supposes, he will spend at some desk in MACV Headquarters near Saigon. What did the troops call it, tolerating the presence of the officious colonels and majors from MACV who were always flying down to look at the Force? Hollywood West? It was as if one of the five sides of the Pentagon had been lifted out of its foundation, flown halfway around the world, and been deposited—airconditioning, coffee shops, uptight staff officers and all—in the war zone. That's where Lemming will send him, he reckons, calling one of his cronies, telling him he's got a colonel who can't cut it as a commander, asking him to find Robertson a place. Maybe in G-4? He could supervise the distribution of jockstraps to the troops, or perhaps oil of citronella, responsible for the whole expeditionary force. For the General is certain to relieve him; he does not brook insolence, and the Knapp after-action report, which Robertson has endorsed and dispatched directly to the General, is nothing if not insolent. True, but superbly insolent.

Robertson lies in his bunk and stares up at the overhead, too tired to sleep easily. He calculates the time and sequence. The report will go direct to the General (as soon as the mail ship can take off, when the rain stops); it'll be in his hands by 1830. Lemming will finish his drink, excuse himself in his courtly way, drive from the General's mess to the helipad at Division, and fly out to the *Samson*. Then there'll be the inevitable showdown. He'll be out here by 1845. It won't be a shouting match: just those deadly eyes trained on him, several quiet words, and it will be done. Perhaps even the promise of a medal for a sweetener. Robertson turns onto his stomach, dozes.

There is suddenly a hand on his shoulder, importunate and nervous. He frowns against the light streaming in from the study and sees his friend Claiborn's face staring down at him. No need to ask what is meant, for Claiborn, sensing what is to come, says: "We're behind you, Colonel." Robertson points at the study. Is he in there? The Major nods. "Tell him I'll be right out." Claiborn leaves, closing the door behind him. Robertson gets up, splashes cold water on his face, puts on his fatigue jacket, and steps out into the study.

There is no noise. The rain has stopped. The sunset can be seen through the open porthole. No one is in the study but Lemming, sitting on the table facing the door of Robertson's stateroom, staring at him with a look of dedicated hatred as he walks out. He says nothing, waiting for Robertson to start talking, perhaps half-expecting a quavering apology. But that is not in Colonel Robertson's mind. He has another plan.

"It's nice of you to come down, Sir. I have an idea you'd like to see the wounded down below." He glances pointedly at his watch. "The dispensary closes to visitors in fifteen minutes. It'd mean so much to the troops if you'd say a few words to them."

Lemming doesn't want particularly to see the wounded—plenty of time for that later—but he is outflanked and knows it. "Alright," he says amicably.

He ambles over to the passageway door (he is not to be hurried) and calls for his aide. "Terwilliger, what'd you bring down in the way of decorations? You got some bronze stars for valor and some purple hearts? Colonel Robertson and I are going below to talk to some of Colonel Plowman's wounded." He turns to Robertson. "Plowman's wounded come here, don't they?"

"Yes, Sir. They come here."

Terwilliger pats the canvas kit bag slung over his shoulder so Lemming can hear the clinks of the medals inside, and the three of them snake their way together down through the ship, naval ratings and soldiers popping tight against the bulkheads as they recognize the two stars on the General's cap. "How are ya? How are ya? Good to see ya," he says to them. Just above the waterline, under the wardroom, is a beautifully equipped dispensary, cool, shining and antiseptic. A corpsman in the waiting-room looks up from his *Cavalier* and comes to attention as the officers enter.

"Unnerstand you've got some of my boys down here," Lemming says. "Like to see 'em for a minute or two."

Some of my boys, Robertson thinks. The bastard. He follows the General into the ward.

On either side of the narrow ward are beds, ten to a side. Lemming walks all the way to the far bulkhead, letting the troops see him—those that are awake and able to see—turns around, and heads slowly back up the aisle, stopping in front of each bunk. The first trooper has had a kneecap blown off by a booby-trap, and his leg is extended on an aluminum support at an angle of 45 degrees to the mattress. The soldier, sensing the General's business, has laid his newspaper on his chest and is propping himself up on his elbows when Lemming stops before him.

"How're you feeling, son?"

"Good, Sir, real good."

"How'd you get hit?"

"I got it jumping off the ramp of a tango boat. They had command-detonateds on the bank."

"Give you any pain now?"

"Nah, not now, Sir. No pain."

Lemming nods, drops his eyes, smiles. "Where're you from, son?"

"Owatonna, Minnesota, Sir."

"Ah, yeah, that's beautiful country out there. One of my boys goes to college in Minnesota."

"Yes, Sir? Where's that, the University?"

"No, Carleton College."

The soldier nods at the General. "Kid's got some smarts, huh?"

"Ah, he's a worker."

"Beats working here, I guess."

"I guess it does." The string is up; there is a long pause in the conversation, neither Lemming nor the PFC from Owatonna knowing how to continue. Finally the General turns to Captain Terwilliger and asks him for a purple heart and a bronze star with "V". The aide hands them over, each decoration already fitted out with a stationer's clip to save the General fumbling with a catch and pin. Lemming moves around to the side of the bed, leans over the soldier, and attaches the decorations to his pajama pocket, saying, "Well, we're real proud of you, real proud."

"Thank you, Sir."

Real proud, Robertson thinks. The General says "really proud," or "really delighted" when he talks to his staff officers. With the troops he gets in that homey Shenandoah touch. *Real proud*. The man's a master.

The party moves off, down between the bunks, working its way back toward the waiting-room. The same conversational sequence is repeated over and over, the words changed slightly so that the soldiers in adjacent bunks don't catch the routine of it. How're you feeling, son? How'd you get hit? Where you from? Biloxi? Moline? Salt Lake? Laramie? Great country. Man could settle down there and live real good. We're real proud. Captain Terwilliger, please? Thanks. We're real proud. Goddamit these kids are lions, aren't they, Robertson?

At last they come to two bunks partitioned off from the others. Neither of their occupants is conscious. General Lemming reaches down for the clipboard hanging from the crank at the foot of the first bunk and reads the medical history of Paul Compella since 2345 last night. "This one's critical, General," the doctor advises, adding in a voice just above a whisper, "I don't know if he's going to make it. Bad head wound."

"Why wasn't he sent to 42nd Surg? Maybe he'd be in Japan by now."

"He was operated on last night around 0300. We don't want to move him yet."

"Is there brain damage?"

"Extensive brain damage."

Goddamn shame, Lemming thinks, but says nothing further. Again he looks over at Terwilliger, takes the decorations, and clips them onto Compella's blanket, staring at the soldier's face. It reminds him of the face of a male nun, the adhesive taut across his forehead. He turns and looks at Colonel Robertson, pursing his lips as he shakes his head. Real slow-like, Robertson thinks.

"I think I saw this kid once, Robertson. Didn't he used to do briefings at Division with Major Sorenson?"

"Very briefly, yes, Sir. Only for a day or two, I think. He'd only been in-country for a week."

"Yeah, that's right. Damn shame. Nice-looking boy."

"Yes, Sir, real fine kid."

"Well," the General turns back to the surgeon, "notify Colonel Robertson and me as to any changes in his condition."

"Of course, General."

The party leaves the ward.

Down at the far end the soldier from Owatonna without a kneecap has been listening and watching the officers' progress through the ward. From time to time he has reached out to his buddy in the next bunk, making whispered comments about it. Now, as the door closes behind Lemming, he catches his friend's eye again.

"Fucking prick," he says.

It is done without eloquence, without apparent anger, without remorse. Colonel Sadler is the name of the new brigade commander. Robertson's executive officer and Major Claiborn will stay on for the time being. It takes time to break in a new CO in the riverine environment, sometimes too much time, doesn't it, Robertson? The Colonel will get his Legion of Merit and the General likes to think he has enough drag up in Saigon to get him something decent at MACV. Hell, he's only got, what? Six months left in-country? Perhaps he could meet his wife in Honolulu for a week before reporting up to Saigon. Make a fresh start.

"But I'm obliged to warn you, Robertson, that insubordination of this sort may not be tolerated by other commanders. The airmobile company you didn't get went to Morton's brigade, and Morton's got a major fight on his hands right now. The assets weren't wasted. And I can't say that I think your casualties were significantly greater in Kien Hoa than they would have been if you had had helicopters."

The *post hoc* variation, Robertson thinks, sensing that Lemming already believes it.

"I'm not going to ruin you on your OER, either. No, you're not getting a clean bill-of-health. In fact it's unlikely that you'll ever command anything again. But you'll survive if you learn this lesson. A star is not out of the question.

"I've got to go. I haven't relieved many commanders, George, and I've never done it with malice. We've got a mission in this war, and anything which creates friction, slows down its accomplishment, has got to be eliminated. A commander who drags his heels is infinitely more dangerous to us than the VC."

"What's the mission, General?"

But Lemming ignores him, shakes Robertson's hand before Robertson can withdraw it, and is gone.

No hard feelings, you understand.

FOUR

Departures

THE SOLDIER

YES. Why do we all, seeing of a soldier, bless him? bless
Our redcoats, our tars? Both of these being, the greater part,
But frail clay, nay but foul clay. Here it is: the heart,
Since, proud, it calls the calling manly, gives a guess
That, hopes that, makes believe, the men must be no less;
It fancies, feigns, deems, dears the artist after his art;
And fain will find as sterling all as all is smart,
And scarlet wear the spirit of war there express.

Mark Christ our King. He knows war, served this soldiering
    through;
He of all can reeve a rope best. There he bides in bliss
Now, and seeing somewhere some man do all that man can
    do,
For love he leans forth, needs his next must fall on, kiss,
And cry "Oh Christ-done deed! So God-made-flesh does too:
Were I come o'er again" cries Christ "it should be this."

GERARD MANLEY HOPKINS

★ 20 ★

Headquarters, Twelfth Infantry Division in Vietnam
0850 Hours, 10 April 1968

ON the walls of General Lemming's office, behind the great desk, are patterns of pale rectangles, the impressions left by pictures and framed citations and personal maps and plaques removed this morning after hanging there for fourteen months. Sergeant Kowalski has taken them down, wrapped them in tissue paper, and packed them. He has already polished the desk once more, removing the clutter for the last time. Into the footlockers go the bibelots: the elephants and the bronze Balinese dancers, the cigarette boxes and swagger sticks, the folders and calendars and pads—all the souvenirs. The polished artillery-shell ashtrays will stay behind, the thoughtful gifts of one general to another.

Lemming likes indoor places, remembers their ambience, their smells, the way the light angles through the windows onto their floors and furniture. He will particularly miss this office, from which he has commanded what some officers have told him was the best fighting division in Vietnam. A lot got done here. What a pleasure it was, working with Colonel Murphy, with Crauford and Terwilliger and the young battalion commanders who came by to talk modestly of their tactics and their body-counts. All of it was pleasure, all the activity that went on in this room—even, he reflects, the things that annoyed him at the time. For in all the activity he was at stage-center, could control things—the deployment of battalions, the giving of solatium, the sequence and direction of a reporter's questions, the way his staff carried out his orders, the building of base camps, the formulation of new strategies.

Of course some blood's been spilled here (not as it was up in the Nineteenth Division, where the headquarters people were actually killed and wounded in rocket attacks), but that blood was not wasted. No. You cut out dead tissue so that healthy tissue might grow. You destroyed some careers in the process, careers just beginning to fulfill their early promise: but better here, he thinks, here in the Twelfth Division while they're still light colonels and majors than somewhere else later on. Other careers have been made, by the bold stroke of a pen or the attachment of a medal to a deserving breast. His own has flourished. He has orders to the *Strategic Welfare Studies Center* at Fort Cuhlman, where he will be commandant and director, and he will go there as a lieutenant general.

But first there will be a long leave in Sequenoy. The Shenandoah is ripening now in the early spring. The rolling meadows are green and spongy; the young colts are beginning to skitter along the fences, over the hills. There will be time to sit by the great rough-stone fireplace and dip into the military history published in the last eighteen months, time to walk along the route of Jackson's Army of the Shenandoah, perhaps even to write an article or two about the Vietnam War. And time to love the good ample woman who has been his wife for thirty-four years. And still more time to attend the graduations of sons and nephews. "This is General Lemming," the headmasters and professors will say, introducing him around to the parents and alumni. Not cornflakes manufacturer Lemming, or Company Director Lemming, or country lawyer Lemming, but "my good friend, *General* Lemming—you probably saw him on the ABC Evening News, did you not? Katherine, you must be so proud, so happy to have him home safe. We all slept better knowing you were leading our kids over there, General. Perhaps you'll say a few words to the graduates?"

Kowalski and the Chief-of-Staff and the aide come and go, carrying things out, putting a few more papers in the "In" basket, working quietly so as not to disturb him. They correctly imagine he wants to be alone with his thoughts before he goes out to be decorated. General Paunce has already been briefed at length: he is ready to take command of the Lionheads. For Lemming it is now only a matter of clearing the last papers from his desk, of signing the last pieces of paper.

His affectations to the contrary, paperwork has never really bothered him. It gives him a sense of detailed control. He has been signing letters of condolence now for a long time, never blinking at the invariable last line of the form letter: "We who are left will carry on the struggle to bring freedom to Vietnam." That is sufficient placebo. In deep mourning you don't think about the politics too carefully. And he has been writing and endorsing letters of recommendation and officers' efficiency reports for years. In his benevolent mood of this morning he makes no written demurrer to the extravagant language used to describe the activities of his officers by those writing their efficiency reports. What the hell? But, Christ, you could name a fleet of battleships after the qualities his commanders and staff perceive in their subordinates: "intrepid, brilliant, valiant, indefatigable, invincible, gallant . . ."

On the efficiency reports are tiny little men standing tall. One little man stands at the top. Under him two more little men. Under them four. Under them thirteen more. Sixty. Thirteen. Four. Two. One. If the officer you are rating is a great friend, or if you know him to have been a great soldier, or if it eases your conscience to give him a handsome boost, then make a check next to the one little man at the top. He stands alone. And, odd thing, all the efficiency reports he goes through this morning have checks next to the one little man at the top, standing tall.

He looks up, watching the motes tumble in the shafts of light from the window. It'll be crowded at the Chief-of-Staff's desk in a few years. All his officers seem to be bound for the top.

He shrugs, signs the last of them, turns to other

papers. Combat after-action reports, draft "Lessons-Learned pamphlets" (a PET milk can makes an excellent booby-trap, if properly configured), brigade and battalion SITREPS, District Intelligence Briefing abstracts, body-count mimeos, weapons stats. He initials them all with his big GSL. *I have seen and wish to make no obtrusion.* On to other papers. He reads through the personal notes from his friends, agreeing easily with their testimonials to his achievements as Commanding General. Without looking up he reaches over to the "In" box, feels for more papers, finds only one.

We all slept better knowing you were leading our kids over there. He slides the last paper in front of him. Shit. A Congressional. It is a letter dated 5 April, from the Office of the Chief of Legislative Liaison. The usual inquiry about a soldier, routinely sent across his desk by his own request, like all Congressionals. They can get a bit sticky, but he likes to keep up with this sort of thing, flatters himself that he knows more about what goes on in his Division than any other commander. What are the troops complaining about? Lots of times their complaints are legitimate ones that the company commanders might have, should have taken care of themselves.

The language of these letters is always careful and restrained. Congressmen do not as a rule write generals in the field on such matters; rather, they channel their inquiries through a colonel in Washington. The colonel and his assistants gently pose the questions to the leaders in the field: "Why Specialist Four Herbert has written no letter home in his three months in Vietnam; why PFC Johnston is sent to the field despite his severe foot diseases; why Specialist Five Donovan wasn't transferred to MACV Headquarters; why PFC Paul Compella, deceased, was not promptly med-evacked out of the combat zone to a hospital with facilities better able to treat his wounds. It is felt by the deceased member's parents that such procedure would have saved the member's life."

Compella, Compella. Lemming bites at the eraser on his pencil, trying to remember the soldier, trying to connect the name with a face. Wait a minute. Yes, now he's got it: the handsome soldier on the boat, wounded in the Kien Hoa Sweep . . .

"Excuse me, General, COMUSMACV's chopper is five minutes out."

"Is the ceremony all laid on?"

"Yes, Sir. Are you ready? We've got your stuff loaded on your C and C, ready to go."

"Thanks, Chuck. I guess we'd better get down to the ceremony."

"Looks like you're leaving a clean desk for General Paunce."

"The least I can do for the poor bastard."

"He's got a tough act to follow, Sir."

"Thanks, Chuck, it means a lot to hear you say that. But he'll have you here to keep him straight. He'll do alright."

"Thank you, Sir."

"There's one item. A Congressional. Parents want to know why a trooper didn't get proper medical treatment, one of those."

"You want Mason to draft a reply?"

"Yeah. Good. He's done a lot of those. You sign for Paunce. Don't start him off with a Congressional."

"Yes, Sir."

General Lemming stands up, tidies his jungle-fatigue jacket, carefully wraps the pistol belt around his waist. He walks slowly toward the office door.

"I'll miss this place. You ready, Chuck? You did a great job here. You won't be forgotten . . ."

"Thank you, Sir." He starts to say something more, but realizes his voice will crack if he does.

"Jesus Christ, don't be maudlin. Let's get outside."

★ 21 ★

Gallo Memorial Cemetery, Torrington, Connecticut
0930 Hours (EST), 10 April 1968

TO people from other parts of the country Connecticut seems to arrange itself into two societies: suburban New York City—Darien, New Canaan, Westport, Ford Country Squires, the "Consciousness II" liberalism of a commuting society living over its head; beyond this, beyond a circle with perhaps a sixty-mile radius pivoting on Manhattan, the rolling spare Berkshires—Litchfield County, poets' retreats, the boys' boarding schools. There is more to the state than this. There is, for example, the grimy Naugatuck Valley, running south to north across the western part of the state like an ugly scar, a skein of old milltowns—Derby, Seymour, Naugatuck, Ansonia, Waterbury, Torrington, Winsted—industrialized communities of third-generation Italian and Polish Americans. The Connecticut war dead are mainly of this culture. For it is not Hotchkiss School or Greenwich or Pierson College that supplies the one-one bravos to the infantry battalions in Vietnam.

And in Torrington a Requiem Mass has just been sung in St. Peter's Church, and a funeral procession of perhaps seventy-five cars is moving slowly off the inlet road to another, narrower, driveway. Mrs. Raymond Compella, in the leading limousine, sees the awning ahead, three men standing under it, two of them priests and another in military uniform. The figures are motionless, their hands identically fig-leafed over their topcoats. They watch the line of cars move toward them, their heads bobbed forward so that they seem to be looking up at the procession. On Mrs. Compella's right is her husband Raymond; and in front of them their two daughters sit facing them. No one says anything. In the front seat Frank Ruselli, godfather of the deceased, nods over at the awning, and the driver pulls up fifteen yards away. Mrs. Compella is dully conscious of the car's heat curling up around her ankles.

Slowly the family gets out on either side of the car and walks toward the awning and the gravesite and stands across from the priest. It is a gray day, gray and windlessly cold enough for the breaths of the mourners to show against their topcoats. Blotches of old filthy snow are caked and layered around the bases of the tombstones where the early spring sunlight has never been. Mrs. Compella is vaguely aware of the asymmetry of the graveyard skyline: crypts, tombs, a mausoleum, headstones set randomly and crowded all around. The larger the stone the less the love, she thinks. The priest looks over at her with a determined but infinite tenderness, an expression she somehow connects only with the eyes of the anaestheseologist looking down at her the morning Paul was born. So rapid has been the passage of years. The city had the same mayor then as it does now.

What was it she had read years ago, an account of Polish Jews going in groups to be shot into a trench, one of the girls saying to a soldier, over and over, "twenty years old . . . twenty years old." And now Paul, nineteen. The priest reads from his Missal. She remembers her son in the New Haven Arena three years ago, fiercely quick, eyes shooting sideways, head up, the right hand knowing, controlling the dribble as he brings the ball up court in a delirium of screaming and heat: Torr-ing-ton! His calf muscles flexed over his socks as he pushes off, elbow cocked, hand over the back of his head, "Shoot! Shoot!" and the ball springing off supple fingers and then arcing down from the rafters, its flight broken only by the webbing of the net.

How could he know what he was doing? Was there even a civics class at Torrington High? Time slides by in a changed expression: Paul at ten, holding his mother's hand at this very graveyard, the same hand her husband clasps now. Her mother's funeral.

She has not heard what the priest was saying. Now he blesses the casket, two hundred mourners watching in a stillness broken only by his toneless voice and the drone of a plane miles away. A flag folded into a cushion is placed in her hands. Some begin to turn away, to walk to their cars, and suddenly what she has dreaded begins to happen.

A voice cracking like a caw: "Please wait, wait . . . I knew him. He was vice-president of his class when

I became principal. I want to say . . . he was a good and a kind boy . . . When I walked into the classroom the first day I was at the high school he came up to me and shook my hand. He introduced me. He always did things like that and I loved him for it." Mr. Lewis in his grief is conscious of his audience, unhappy in their taciturnity, in knowing what their bumper stickers advertise, that one of them last week had told him Martin Luther King's murderer should only have to pay a fine for "shooting coon out of season," that the older mourners have soldiered across Europe in the infantry and regard Paul's death as somehow just and as an honor to the city.

"For what, for what? . . . This hideous war . . . Is there a purpose? . . . What did he die for? For nothing? What did he do?"

Frances Compella has taken everything on faith all her life. Vietnam, certainly; her husband had explained it to her driving back from Bradley Field the day their son left them. See, if we don't stop them there they'll get Jap-an, which is our ally now, and Australia. How'd you like to see them on the Golden Gate Bridge shooting children? That's the way these people are, and you have to draw a line somewhere and we drew it *there.* No one else did, so we had to. Don't worry about him. He's smart. There's a picture in *Life* of this surgical ward they attach to the bottom of a helicopter and fly it right in to where they are. I think it was only 2 percent they don't save. No, Frances, Paul's no problem. Don't worry about it. A year from now we'll have him back here and be proud of him.

She knew he would be killed. Paul, at 5′ 8″, *challenging*, the announcer kept repeating. "Compella challenges Paine, who is 6′ 3″, dribbles up to him and shoots over his head." "Compella challenges Gregg with a high inside fastball and snaps it over the plate." Outside stadiums he didn't challenge anyone. But *there* he would, she knew. Thus he would die. No Communist would stride down the Golden Gate Bridge looking for children to shoot. No Red would get onto the island of Japan. She tried to make herself think he was safe, tried by acts of faith. But they never became rooted conviction, were choked from the start. She tried to believe what he was doing was somehow worthy, and sometimes fresh eddies of conviction had carried her along: a report of a bombed orphanage in Saigon, a picture in the papers of a tiny yellow child in New York for surgery and a trip to F.A.O. Schwartz, Paul's few letters—confident and disordered.

But it was no use. Her acts of faith were stunted growths, and on April 10th at the funeral only the thinnest stems connect her with them. Mr. Lewis cuts through them now as with a razor.

"For what?"

Now there remained not even that consolation to which she might have come to accommodate herself through the months and turning seasons ahead. No belief to cling to, no reason why to be believed, no certitudes. Only her husband now with his arm around her waist, taking her back to the limousine.

★ 22 ★

LET us decorate our General, in front of his own Headquarters. He is in position already, standing in an almost geriatric parody of what he was taught at The Citadel thirty-nine years ago, his jungle-fatigue jacket hanging off his shoulders as if they were a broken wooden hanger. In spite of themselves, his staff takes an odd pleasure in seeing him like this, at attention, waiting for *his* superior. All the mornings of the long months past, precisely at 0725, they have come to attention as he walked through the Division office on his way to be briefed, passing their desks without looking at them, only absently saying "morning, morning," already absorbed in the challenges of the new day.

He is at attention on the sandy fresh topsoil in front of Division. Somewhere miles away a plane drones. It is, as always, hot and windy, and the lapels and shirt-tails of the General's fatigue jacket flap in the breeze.

205

From where the staff and subordinate commanders are standing it is difficult to make out his face. The visor of his green baseball cap keeps his eyes and forehead hidden, but underneath, inside the shade, they imagine those eyes of his, corvine, deadly deep-blue, without remorse, not following the progress of the awards party as it moves slowly toward him.

The General who will decorate him with the Distinguished Service Medal is an august shuffling presence, a U.S. Grant in faded green poplin. He makes his left-face awkwardly in the sand, and his aide hands him the decoration which he has carried—yes, on a cushion. From somewhere behind the assembled staff, flinty and disembodied, a voice begins a familiar incantation:

> By order of the President, the Distinguished Service medal is presented to Major General George Simpson Lemming, 040618, United States Army, for exceptionally meritorious service while serving in a position of great responsibility as Commanding General, Twelfth Infantry Division, from February 1967 to April 1968. During General Lemming's tenure as commanding general, the Division, largely as a result of his intrepid and imaginative leadership, achieved unequaled success in furtherance of its mission to eliminate Viet Cong insurgency in its assigned area of operations. It established and developed four major base camps, created a logistical base capable of sustaining its manifold combat and civic action operations, successfully conducted its search-and-clear mission against an aggressive and capable enemy, inaugurated a program of civic-action operations which have brought new friendship and understanding between American forces and the people and armed forces of the Republic of South Vietnam, and by unfailingly skillful airmobile, riverine, and conventional operations cut major

enemy supply routes in its area of responsibility. During the period of General Lemming's command the Division and attached forces conducted combat operations resulting in 9456 enemy killed, captured 820 Viet Cong and North Vietnamese soldiers, accounted for 190 Hoi Chanh, destroyed 12,230 structures known to have been built or occupied by the enemy, captured 12 tons of enemy documents, and conducted 4000 separate civic-action operations ranging from the rendering of simple medical treatment of indigenous personnel to the construction of 32 new elementary schools and 8 hospitals.

The Twelfth Infantry Division particularly distinguished itself during the enemy's recent TET offensive and in the weeks immediately afterwards. In a time of great crisis it stood firm against the repeated onslaughts of the enemy infantry, seized the initiative from him, and eventually routed him from the Division area of responsibility. General Lemming personally directed and coordinated many of the operations of his assigned maneuver elements during this period, repeatedly exposing himself to hostile fire, inspiring commanders and troops alike by his visionary leadership, unremitting courage, and great stamina.

General Lemming's service as commanding General, Twelfth Infantry Division, is in keeping with the highest traditions of American military service and reflects great credit upon himself, the United States Army, and the United States of America.

By direction of the Secretary of the Army, /s/ Stanley R. Resor.

A few crackles from the loudspeaker, and it is shut off. Now the theater commander has clipped the medal to the General's pocketflap, and he stands back a foot or so and their hands grope, as they study each other's faces, grope and lock and pump. Nelson and Collingwood. MacArthur and Wainwright. It is an intensely personal moment for them both, a mutual, relieved affirmation that what each knows the other to have been doing for the past thirty-five years is worthy and true and of good report. Now the senior general's left hand goes out and clasps Lemming's elbow. They are smiling at each other, hard, as if proclaiming together that, by God, some things *are* sacred in this collapsing world of 1968, and friendship among brave warriors is one of them. The small band to their left breaks the quiet with a Sousa march and the generals awkwardly turn, lurch into a jerky cadenced step, and stride together off the field.

Afterword

Except for Paul Compella, all the characters who figure prominently in the narrative survived their tours in Vietnam.

George Simpson Lemming is at Fort Cuhlmann with the war studies group to which he was assigned in April 1968. He is hopeful that he will be reassigned as Supreme Commander, Allied Powers in Europe. His book, *Memoirs of An Infantry General* (nothing in it to prejudice his chances for the SHAPE job), was published in January 1970, and a short excerpt from it may be found in Appendix II of this book.

Charles Murphy, Lemming's Chief of Staff, is a brigadier and an assistant division commander at Fort Lewis. His oldest son was caught blowing grass at the Virginia Military Institute, dismissed by the authorities, and is now a PFC in Germany.

George Robertson is living off his pension and his

wife's money at Sea Island, Georgia. He has become a great reader of W. H. Auden and Thomas Love Peacock.

Charles Claiborn gained early promotion to lieutenant colonel. Then, against the dire warnings of Infantry Branch, he turned down his assignment to the War College in favor of a tour of duty as deputy professor of military science at Columbine University, Cranston, Montana.

Philip Knapp, Robertson's former plans officer, is involved in the defense of Daniel Ellsberg. The firm of Churchill, Berman, Garrison and Hunt, Los Angeles, considers his services worth $35,000 a year.

Alden Jacobs failed to secure advancement in the naval service and is a buyer for Chipp, Clothiers. His sloop *Invicta* recently finished fourth in the Newport-Bermuda race.

The new gymnasium at Torrington High School is called Compella Memorial Gymnasium, and Paul Compella's bronze star was melted into the wall plaque soldered underneath the press box.

Appendix I

LEMMING, George Simpson. b. 29 October 1912, Roanoke, Virginia; son of Jesse Simpson LEMMING (med. Dr.) and Ruth TALIAFERRO LEMMING; educ Roanoke local schools; Woodberry Forest School, Virginia (grad. 1929); The Citadel, Charleston, S.C. (maj crs study: Civil Engineering; B.S., 1933). Comm. 2d Lt, Inf, 5 June 1933; lv absence June '33–Jul '34 for rsns health; grad Inf Ofcs Indoctr. Crs, Ft. Benning, Ga, Febr 1935—Distinguished Honor Graduate; comd plat 1st Bn 67th Inf Regt, Ft. Benning, Mar '35–Jan '36; S-4, same, Jan '36–Nov '36; Aide-de-Camp to Maj Gen Withers ROCKACRE, Hq 1st USA, Governors' Island, N.Y., to Dec 1939. Prom capt. Dec 1939; Jan 1940–Nov 1940 asgd C.O., Co "B" 1st Bn 67th Inf, Ft. Benning; Sp Advisor 41st N.G. Division, Tennessee, Nov 1940–Sept 1941; Adv Inf Crs, Ft. Benning, Sept 1941–June 1942; prom Maj May 1942; asgd X.O., 2d Bn 54th Inf Regt, 21st Div. Jul 1942; Partic Opn TORCH as S-3, same Bn; wounded Tunisia, Jan '43; Sp Projects Officer, Hq, USSComEur, Washington, May '43–Febr 1944; prom Lt Col May 1944, asgd C.O. 1st Bn, 12th Inf, 27th Inf Div; partic Normandy Invasion w/ unit; wounded 1 July, St-Exupery, France; prom Col 15 Nov 1944, asgd C.O. 12th Inf, 27th Inf Div, 18 Nov 1944. Comd same to Oct 1945; USC&GSC, June

211

1946–June 1947; PMS, The Citadel, June 1947–June 1951; reasgd C. O. 7th Inf Regt, 7th Inf Div, ROK, to May 1952; reasgd C/S, same Div to April 1953; St and Fac, USC&GSC, June 1953–July 1955; stud. Univ Penna, July 1955–Feb 1957 (M.A. in I.R.); Hq. SHAPE, J-3 Plans, May 1957–Aug 1959; SpMil Asst, SecArmy, Sept 1959–Jul 1961; prom Brig Gen, AUS, Jul 1961; Asst Div Cdr 10th Div Sept '61–Dec '62; Chairman, Tactical Concepts Eval and Projection Comm, Ft. Bragg, N.C., to Jan '64; Asst Dep C/S, OCDCSPER, Wash DC, Mar '64–Jan '66; prom Maj Gen, AUS, Mar 1966 and reasgd Indiv Inf Tng Directorate, CONARC, US (to Jan 1967). C.G., 12th Inf Div, RVN, from Febr 1967 to pres.

Aw and dec: DSM; SStar w/2 OLC; LegMerit w/ 1/OLC; BrStar w/ "V"; AirMedal; ArComMedal; Croix de Guerre w/ palm; Order of Gall (Lux); C.I.B. (US); Purple Ht w/ 1 OLC; AmDef Med; NatDef Med; Eur Vict Med w/ 4B.S.; UN Svc Med; Korean Svc Medal.

Organizations: Mason; Kts of St Str; KA; AUSA; Assoc MinSoldiersCols

Publications: "Technical Liabilities of the ONTOS," ARMY, Jan 1954; "Integrated Tactical Nuclear Systems in Defense of W. Europe"—M.A. thesis, dir, Robt Strauz-Hupé, Univ Penn, Jan 1957; w/ Col. Jaspar Stuart: "Military Usages of the AD-4C, ARMY, May 1960"; "The Legacy of Douglas MacArthur," sp to VFW mtg, Detroit, 1962, repr in COMBAT, Dec '62; "Is West Point Troglodytic?", NY TIMES, Nov 21, 1967.

Family: m June 1934 Katherine MacBride GARRISON, Richmond Va. iss: George Simpson Lemming Jr, b. 1949 (student); Thomas Forrest Lemming, b. 1953; perm res: Sequenoy Farms, RFD # 2, Sequenoy, Virginia. HArriman 5-4651.

—*Flett's Register of Professional Soldiers of NATO Signatories* (Jan. 1968)

Appendix II

An extract from *Memoirs of an Infantry General,* G.S. Lemming (Kingsley and Thurman, Chicago, 1970, p. 171)

". . . the brigade commanders fought like wolves for the very limited numbers of helicopters available to support their operations. The River Brigade's feelings were frequently bruised because, in their judgment, helicopters were not assigned to their operational control as often as they should have been.

On the other hand, they had large numbers of troop-carrying boats, bravely and efficiently manned by USN personnel assigned to the Mobile Riverine Force. The other brigades had nothing in the way of organic transportation. On many occasions I was forced to assign airmobile companies to the other brigades, even when the River Brigade had hard intelligence inputs. Usually my instincts were proved right in the event. . . .

Moreover, the River Brigade's own casualties were not materially worsened, during their operations from the boats, because they had no helicopters. . . .

All three brigade commanders in the time frame December 1967 to April 1968 were gifted tacticians and loyal subordinates."